What the critics are saying...

Rating 5.0 Sensuality 5.0! "*Nemesis of the Garden* was an absolutely charming romp, hilarious, sensual and sooo romantic. Just the right cure to cheer you up on a depressing, gray winterday." ~ *Ha Mon Boudoir*

Four angels! "Reading *Ms. Starr's Divine Interventions Series* is like revisiting old friends. If you like books with hot, erotic sex and a memorable cast of characters, look to *Cricket Starr's Divine Interventions Series*, especially its latest, *Nemesis in the Garden*." ~ *Tanya Fallen Angel Reviews*

Four hearts! "All this reviewer can do is say BRAVO to *Ms. Starr* for the most exhilarating, exciting finale to this series... Her *Divine Interventions Series* was a delight to read...this reviewer is highly recommending *Nemesis in the Garden* as well as her first books in the series to keep and be enjoyed again and again." ~ *Dawn Love Romances*

"This story was just so creative! I loved the mini-story within a story presented here. It was a complete surprise and made this one a keeper. Pan was one hot hunk of a god, but I also enjoyed the addition of the relationship between Eos and Astraios—what a loving couple they were! ...know that all you mythology buffs out there will get a kick out of this one!" ~ *Joyce Driver Coffee Time Romance*

This is a nice spin on the relationships of the Greek deities and the spicier elements will keep you engaged and wanting more of *Ms. Starr's* work." ~ *Jacqueline eCataRomance Reviews*

Cricket Starr

Nemesis of the Garden

An Ellora's Cave Romantica Publication

www.ellorascave.com

Divine Intervention: Nemesis of the Garden

ISBN #1419952374

Edited by: Ann Leveille
Cover art by: Syneca

Electronic book Publication: February, 2005
Trade paperback Publication: August, 2005

Warning:

The following material contains graphic sexual content meant for mature readers. *Nemesis of the Garden* has been rated *E-rotic* by a minimum of three independent reviewers.

Ellora's Cave Publishing offers three levels of Romantica™ reading entertainment: S (S-ensuous), E (E-rotic), and X (X-treme).

S-*ensuous* love scenes are explicit and leave nothing to the imagination.

E-*rotic* love scenes are explicit, leave nothing to the imagination, and are high in volume per the overall word count. In addition, some E-rated titles might contain fantasy material that some readers find objectionable, such as bondage, submission, same sex encounters, forced seductions, etc. E-rated titles are the most graphic titles we carry; it is common, for instance, for an author to use words such as "fucking", "cock", "pussy", etc., within their work of literature.

X-*treme* titles differ from E-rated titles only in plot premise and storyline execution. Unlike E-rated titles, stories designated with the letter X tend to contain controversial subject matter not for the faint of heart.

Also by Cricket Starr:

Divine Interventions 1: Violet Among the Roses
Divine Interventions 2: Echo In the Hall
Memories To Come
The Doll
Two Men and a Lady anthology

Nemesis of the Garden
Divine Interventions

Prologue

The Titan Hyperion stared down from his celestial perch, his gaze fixed on the worlds displayed below. From his throne he could see both Earth and Olympus, the realm of man as well as that of the gods. He muttered under his breath as he watched the actions of those below, their lives playing before him in a million tiny plays.

Their lives, not his. With the other Titans, he'd been given dominion over Titanous, neither part of the Earth, nor Olympus but in another dimension, carved from the celestial heavens. All things considered, he had to admit it was better than being held in the dark underground, as he and his people had been confined so long ago.

After the Titans' last battle with the Olympians, the gods had been "kind" to exile him and his offspring to this place, where there was light instead of eternal darkness. For those who personified the moon, sun, and dawn, it was particularly necessary to their health.

Still, while the view was magnificent, the real estate was meager. Hyperion tried to stretch, only to bang his head on the low ceiling. His home had no room to move about in and he wasn't able to transfer between dimensions the way those of Olympus could. None of the Titans could change their location and even his children, Helios of the sun, Selene of the moon, and Eos, the dawn, had to stay in their celestial realm.

Greedily he watched the gods and goddesses move from Olympus to Earth and back again, playing in the world of humans. Even the lowliest nymph among them had more freedom than his sweet Eos did.

Speaking of which…there she was, that one. Into his view came the nymph, Nemesis, sometimes called Nina. Hyperion watched the small dark-haired beauty with undisguised fury. Nina popped in and out of the world of men with ridiculous ease, while he and his had to spend their lives trapped in this miniscule dimension.

It just wasn't fair. There had to be something Hyperion could do to improve their lot. He could see everything. Maybe he could find some advantage from that.

Hyperion stroked his long white beard. Recently he'd noticed that Nina was spending less time on Earth and more with that hairy-legged excuse for a god, Pan. A lot of time, mostly engaged in carnal delights. He could sometimes hear the sounds of their couplings up here, they were so randy.

He knew Aphrodite had had something to do with this couple getting together. There had been a bow in her hand and then Pan had carried Nina to his bower. Thoughtfully the Titan rubbed his massive jaw. He'd watched the goddess for some time and Aphrodite was forever getting involved with setting up one couple or another. But now she'd messed with Pan, a true god. If the gods found out they were being manipulated there would be war in Olympus and maybe he could turn their unrest to his advantage.

Excited, the Titan leaned forward, watching the pair. A long time ago Pan and Nemesis had spent time as a couple until something had broken them apart, something bad enough to keep them separate for nearly three hundred years in spite of their attraction to each other.

That the attraction still existed was obvious given how happy they were now. Aphrodite's arrow had apparently mended the rift between them.

With a grunt of disgust, Hyperion leaned back again. How could he use Aphrodite's interference when she had actually done them a favor? She'd just claim her intervention was justified and that their love excused everything.

Love excused everything... That was a joke. He'd had enough of new ideas like that. He even had his chief of the guards lusting after his daughter and acting as if being in love justified seeking a princess' hand. Fortunately up to now his girl had shown better sense than to encourage the man. Hyperion grimaced. With so few others to choose from, the longer they were confined here the more likely it was she'd succumb to the man's charm. Eventually he'd lose control of the pair of them.

Frustrated, he pounded his fist on the arm of his throne. They simply had to get free, and it wasn't going by asking as his son Helios seemed to think was possible. If only his people had the power to transfer off this plane. All gods and goddesses, and even minor divinities like Nemesis, had a certain amount of divine power that they used to perform their magic. Titans could use such power but they couldn't manufacture it.

Again Hyperion stroked his beard. Titans couldn't create power, but they could steal it if they got close enough to someone with enough of it. Nemesis was merely a nymph, she wouldn't have enough, and even Pan wouldn't do, but someone like Aphrodite, who had a tendency to poke her perfect nose into other people's affairs...she'd do nicely. But it would take getting a Titan or two on the Olympian plane in some kind of physical form.

Hyperion smiled. Watching the gods for thousands of years had taught him many of their tricks and he knew of one in particular that would be perfect for this job. He even knew which Titans would volunteer for it, he thought wryly.

He had the way and he had the means. Now all he needed was to watch for the opportunity.

Chapter One

Once again Nina dreamed. She stood in Pan's garden and faced Aphrodite, who held the bow and arrow that she, Nina, had stolen. The angry goddess raised the bow and fitted the feathered shaft to it, drawing back and taking careful aim. Cringing, Nina waited for the sharp bite of the arrowhead.

It wouldn't kill her. She'd stolen both arrow and bow from Eros and the worst would be that she'd fall in love with the nearest unattached male. Moments ago that might have been Alex, her sister's man, but he'd just finished declaring his love for Chloe. Fortunately he was now unavailable.

That didn't leave her off the hook, though. She was very much afraid that the person she would end up infatuated with was Pan, the only other man in the garden.

Pan, god of the forests and fields, and seducer of many, many women, including, almost, the attempted ravishment of her own sister. Pan, who swore he'd never fall in love. Pan with his goat-like horns, fleece-covered legs and cock the size of a donkey's.

Nina sighed at the thought of her impending fixation. It was a moot point, anyway. In the deep, dark recesses of her heart she knew she was already desperately in love with the god. What could be worse than being infatuated with someone you were already infatuated with...but who would never return your love?

Too bad it wasn't a real arrow, capable of killing her. Given the alternatives dying sounded pretty good right now.

Nina closed her eyes, hoping for some sort of miracle. Maybe Aphrodite would miss, or change her mind. She cringed when she heard the twang of the bowstring as the goddess let the arrow fly.

"No!" Pan's voice startled her and she opened her eyes just in time to see the god jump in front of her. The arrow entered his back, piercing him through, and ended up in her chest, a sharp pain between her breasts. Shocked, she gazed up into the god's face as it registered first agony from the arrow's passage, then surprise as the shaft melted away, taking the pain with it.

She felt the arrowhead slip from her chest and fall to the ground.

Astonished, she stared at Pan. "You tried to save me." Why would Pan do that, try to prevent injury to her? Was it possible he really cared?

From the other side of the garden came Chloe's voice, talking to her lover. "She wasn't trying to kill you, Alex. It was one of Eros' bows and arrows."

The surprise in Pan's face twisted into fury. "That was one of EROS' ARROWS? How could you be that stupid?" he fumed. "Interfering with the goddess, stealing from Eros. Do you know what you've done? I've been hit with Eros' arrow when I was staring right at you. Now I'm going to be infatuated with you for gods know how long."

Somehow Nina summoned her self-control and met his glare. "No one told you to jump in the way, you big oaf. And for your information, that arrow hit me, too. You think I want you wanting me, or me wanting you? This is as bad for me as it is for you."

He stared down at her, his eyes narrowed into brown slits. "You're a mouthy little wench, aren't you? I probably ought to put that mouth of yours to work doing something useful for a change."

"Oh, yeah?" she challenged. "Like what?"

The next thing she remembered was his mouth on hers, hot and demanding, and the tickle of his beard against her throat. Pan's musk filled her nostrils and lungs, bringing her to instant arousal. She lost the strength in her knees and leaned heavily against him. After that she was across one of his shoulders as he hauled her into his garden bower. Her last memory of the garden was the amused expressions on the faces of her sister and her lover.

Then Pan had tossed her onto his wide bed, not all that gently.

And after that…

* * * * *

…After that he'd fucked her, over and over again, until her throat had been raw with screaming her pleasure. With a moan, Nina jerked out of her dream of that long-ago day, and into the present of Pan's bedroom. It was a rustic space, formed from living trees inside the garden home he kept in Olympus, a place that had been her home for the past five months.

Careful not to disturb her bed partner, Nina settled back on her pillow and tugged the thick wool blanket further up around her neck. The blanket was one of the few manufactured items Pan allowed in his garden, which otherwise held only natural furnishings or items he could coax from living plants through his divine magic.

Her body was still aroused from her dream, but she didn't want to wake Pan just yet. The dim light filtering through the thickly entwined tree branches above told her that it was still a little while until dawn.

It had been five months but she still remembered the most intense sexual experience in her three thousand years of life.

Pan had seemed angry, but his hands had been gentle on her. They'd started with him fulfilling his promise to find something better for her mouth to do. Once inside his bower he'd pulled the loincloth covering his privates from his hips and forced her to her knees before him. He'd held her face between his hands as she'd taken his cock deep into her mouth.

Nina smiled remembering Pan's flavor on her tongue. He'd tasted of man and earth and the forces of nature he embodied.

Once she'd found her rhythm, his hands had sought her nipples, tweaking them through her bra with expertise, sending shockwaves into her clit and pussy. Her nether parts had flooded with arousal and by the time her silk panties had come off they'd been soaked.

Pan had barely seemed to notice how sexy her undergarments were. Instead he'd grumbled about modernized women and their penchant for putting clothing in his way. His only sign of interest in her hundred dollar silk panties had been when he'd ripped them off her and drawn his tongue along the dampened crotch, tasting her essence on the fabric and smacking his lips with relish. Then he'd pushed her back on the bed and opened her legs so he could gather the rest of her womanly dew straight from the source.

It had been several hundred years since the last time she'd had Pan's face between her legs, but Nina hadn't forgotten what a brilliant pussy eater he was. Sometimes it felt like his tongue was a yard long. After lathing her woman's folds it reached far inside her, nearly to her womb. He tickled her clit with his teeth as well, and used his lips and tongue until she was near distraction.

Nina had been brought to orgasm at least twice before he'd decided to move up her body, trailing the head of his cock along her thigh. Staring down into her eyes, he'd fit that thick head of his to her pussy, letting her sense just how big he was before driving home within.

Both of them had groaned then, because he was so big and she was so tight. He'd climaxed immediately, filling her with his hot cum, but hadn't softened at all. Instead the extra fluid had been a welcome lubricant when after a brief rest he'd taken up pounding her furiously. Time after time he'd taken her to paradise, lying on her back with his thick, hot cock deep within her.

When he pulled out of her, he was as hard as when he'd started. Pulling her onto her knees, he'd entered her from behind, rocking her back and forth with his hands on her hips. Leaning over her shoulder, he growled into her ear. He'd spoken soft words about how angry he was at being forced to make love to her, how he'd hated being compelled by Eros' arrow. He told how seriously in trouble she was.

Nina's mind came back to the present, and the still sleeping god beside her. Oh, yeah, she was in seriously big trouble. If only this trouble wouldn't end. She knew it was only a matter of time before the effect of Eros' arrow wore off and Pan returned to his normal, any-nymph-in-a-glade unattached self. She didn't know how long one of Eros' spells was supposed to last, but surely the one on theirs was about to reach some kind of end-date. Oddly enough, so far Pan hadn't shown interest in any other woman, and after five months that was amazing. After all, she thought bitterly, it had only been a week the time before.

She hadn't found any other men of interest either but that was hardly surprising, at least to her. After all, she knew a little secret that no one else did.

Pan was in love with her because Aphrodite had shot him with Eros' arrow of love. She was in love with Pan—just because she was, and had been for a very long time.

Nina had loved Pan for centuries, ever since her first time with him after Psyche's birthday party. She'd become infatuated with the horn-headed, goat-legged god almost at once. In fact it had happened so suddenly, she'd almost suspected there had been something in the ambrosia she'd drunk. She and Pan had spent the better part of a week together before he'd taken off after another female. He'd left her brokenhearted and with a secret penchant for sleeping with a sheepskin pillow that reminded her of Pan's legs.

Turning on her side away from him she ran her foot down his fleece-covered calf, luxuriating in the feel of him. Who said she didn't have good taste in men? Well, many people would argue she didn't, although they wouldn't be talking about her crush on a god. That, at least, she'd managed to keep a secret from the world at large.

She'd had her share of partners over the centuries, even though the other men she'd been to bed with hadn't sparked more than a passing interest in her. Some of it had been business...after all, one couldn't be a star on the number one all-porn-all-the-time adult cable channel without fucking a man occasionally—or frequently. A man or two, or three, occasionally four.

Or fucking the occasional woman, although that was all show as far as she was concerned. Her agent had tried to interest her in doing an all-women film or two, telling her they were very popular with college guys weirded-out by the sight of penises in their porn. She just didn't see the point of sex without penises in one form or another.

But not one of her recent sex partners, male or female, had been able to hold her interest longer than it took to finish having sex with them. In some cases she hadn't even been interested once her own climax had been reached, although she'd learned the hard way that it was better to stay in place until her partner had an orgasm. Some guys really hated it when you left the bed before they got off. Sometimes they got angry, and once she'd even had to use her limited magic to put a man to sleep when he'd gotten violent.

Nina sighed quietly. Human males…fuck them once and they thought they owned you. Next thing you knew they were planning a wedding, kids, and a whole monogamous life with you, all while declaring undying love.

It was enough to seriously annoy a nymph. It wouldn't be so bad if the person who got fixated on you happened to be someone you wanted in return.

Like Pan.

But Pan wasn't someone you could depend on to hold undying monogamous love for anyone. She'd learned that lesson the hard way. No doubt he'd react to her professing love for him with the same contempt she showed the men in her life.

The best thing to do was enjoy being with him while it lasted. When it was over, it would be over, and they'd both go back to their lives. Pan would go back to fucking anything that stayed still long enough, and she'd…well, she'd survive.

She'd done it before—she could do it again. It would be hard, but not impossible.

The warm body behind her stirred and an arm came around her waist to cinch her in close. Nina felt the familiar warm breath of her favorite god on the back of her neck.

"Looks like someone is awake." His hand moved up her body to cup her breast, twisting her nipple with innate skill. As if her nipple was a knob on her passion her arousal turned from simmer to a high boil. Nina couldn't resist a little moan.

The god's voice growled in her ear. "I wonder what I can do with a warm willing nymph in my bed. Assuming you are willing, that is."

He turned her so she was looking up into his face with its piercing eyes and thin goatee. She ran her hand through his curly brown hair, finding the hidden knobs of his short horns.

He'd asked the same question every morning for the past five months, if she was still willing to make love with him. Every day he seemed to expect that she'd have fallen out of love with him as the spell from Eros' arrow had worn off.

"I believe you could do anything you want, Pan. Assuming *you* still want *me*." It was the same answer she'd given every morning, wondering when he'd finally say he'd had enough of her.

And he answered her as he had each of the previous five months of mornings—he kissed her with a kiss that drove all other questions from her head. Pan's mouth covered hers, his lips plying with distracting intent, his tongue engaged in a battle for whose mouth would be probed first. As always she lost the battle and he took possession, tasting the inside of her mouth with long sweeps of his sensuous tongue.

Nina melted under the influence of Pan's kiss. What woman, nymph, or goddess could refuse him anything when he put his wicked mouth to work on her?

Except for Echo. He'd mentioned once how her sister nymph, Echo, now known as Chloe, had been resistant to his kisses, but Pan had attributed it to true love being in effect. Even the god of sensuality couldn't compete with a man who held the heart of his woman.

Secretly Nina had been delighted that Chloe had found her love in Alex and that the man had finally figured out that he, in turn, was in love with her. The last message she'd gotten from the pair was that Chloe and Alex were to be married soon.

Not that any of this was going through her head at the moment. How could it when Pan was kissing her into a place where no thoughts could find purchase? Her mind shut down and left her with nothing but sensation to experience, warm, sensuous sensation, something that had been sadly lacking in her life for many past centuries.

In her life lovers had come and gone, but Pan came, and came, and came, and more often than not made her come with him—assuming she hadn't come sometime before.

She never left Pan's bed unsatisfied. In first couple of weeks of their relationship he'd even gone beyond her stamina and worn her out. She hadn't able to leave the bed for days.

Fortunately she'd gotten a lot stronger and most of the time could keep up with him now. At the moment his hands roamed her body, his lips moving from her mouth to trail kisses down her neck. His legs slid over hers, the soft fleece that covered them caressing her skin. Her legs tingled under its sensuous touch. Even the hardness of his cloven feet as they slid along her feet felt wonderful.

Pan's lips found her nipples, tugging each with practiced care. His hands were gentle as they touched her, particularly in the places she tended to get tender, but he could be demanding when he knew she could take it. He knew her body, almost as well as she did herself. Maybe even better.

It was funny. The first time he'd claimed her, he'd been powerful, intense, a force of nature intent on establishing possession of her. After their first tempestuous night, she'd barely been able to sit down for much of the following day.

Since then Pan had shown more care when he'd had sex with her, almost to the point of being too gentle. She couldn't quite figure him out. The way he acted, it almost didn't seem like the actions of a man under a spell. She could almost believe that he loved her.

Of course he didn't. It was all the fault of Eros' arrow, but how easy it would be to give in to temptation and believe he really meant love in the way he touched her.

But that was impossible. She may be called Nina, but she was Nemesis, former vengeance nymph and enemy of all, and she knew better than to trust anyone or anything, even her own judgment when it came to him. Vengeance nymphs never forgave and they never let love interfere with their lives.

A vengeance nymph would never forget that Pan couldn't possibly care for her.

Or could he? She couldn't help that little whisper of hope.

Still, it didn't much matter if he did or didn't really care for her as long as he kept playing with her most sensitive spots the way he was right now. Nina closed her eyes and gave in to those skilled fingers stroking her sensitive clit, soft folds, and tender pussy. His touch sparked a flame within her—his fingers were steel to her flint, sending sparks everywhere.

Sometimes it surprised her that the bed didn't burst into flames, so hot their sex was. Like now when she lifted her knees and spread them to make it easier for him to touch her.

Pan's hand dove deep within her, curving his fingers and pressing against the inside, reaching for that tiny sensitive spot only he could always find in her. *Gods, he was good at that.* Sometimes she wondered if she would expire from his touch.

It was far more like she'd die from lack of it.

Her little voice spoke again. *If only any of it was real.*

"Tell me what you want, Nina." Pan leaned over her, capturing her gaze with his penetrating eyes.

You – to really love me… Nina bit down on her lips. She couldn't say that aloud. She'd look pathetic when he finally stopped his bespelled infatuation with her. There was no way Nemesis could ever allow herself to look pathetic. Instead Nina forced a sultry smile onto her face. "I want what I always want. Fuck me good and hard, Pan."

An odd look, almost like disappointment, flashed through his eyes. It disappeared as he whispered, "That's what I'll do then."

Pan sat up and grabbed her knees and pulled them further apart. Nina almost felt split in two as he knelt between her thighs. He lifted her ass high in the air to line up with his massive erection, resting the broad head of his cock against her opening. He plunged forward and speared deep within her, filling her as he always did with his hot pulsating cock.

As always, it felt wonderful even as she questioned whether he might someday split her apart entering her this way. She groaned aloud. "Gods, Pan, you can do that forever."

He grinned at her, eyes lively with mischief. "Promise?" he said, and she thought she detected a hint of wistful hope in the question.

Before she could react to his comment, he went into a flurry of strokes that left her breathless and aching for release. She bucked and twisted, her hips held firmly in his hands.

It was a most thorough fucking. Nina could hardly breathe as he filled her, over and over again, his heavy balls bouncing against her ass, still lifted high in the air. As was usual with these early morning fuckings, both reached their climax early. Nina's release came in its normal mind-blowing fashion, her body tensing all over, ripples of sensation dancing from her cock-filled pussy through her body and down her limbs all the way to the tips of her toes and fingers. She screamed his name in a long banshee-like wail.

Moments later Pan tensed over her and growled, his hands hard on her hips, and Nina could feel his cum explode within her, his cock pulsing and pumping it deep into her womb.

At the peak of his climax, Pan leaned forward to stare into her eyes, his gaze intensely sensual and possessive. Her name was on his lips, his voice harsh and guttural. As usual he called her Nemesis instead of her adopted name but Nina couldn't work up the energy to protest. She was too wrung out to feel indignant about anything, much less what name he called her in his passion.

Still on his knees, Pan pulled her off the bed and into his arms, holding her close to him. His mouth slanted over hers as if through his kiss he could claim her and mark her as his. As always, Nina swooned a little at his sensuous kiss.

Cock still buried deep within her, Pan lay on the bed, cradling her body close to him, and they lay still, replete, and for the brief moment sated. Not for long, Nina knew. Their early morning couplings were always like this, intense and fast. Each morning Pan took possession of her as if claiming her for the first time, unable to control his need for sex.

During the day when they made love, it was with a hint of distraction, the pair of them playing hooky from their usual activities. A little bit of fun between the responsibilities they both had.

But in the evening their lovemaking was slower, more relaxed. It had become the coupling of two people comfortable with each other. They lay together for hours sometimes, touching, stroking, and using hands, fingers, mouths, feet and hooves to give each other pleasure. When the last groan and moan had sounded, they would hold each other all through the Olympian night, too tired from their exertions to do anything other than sleep.

It had been the best five months she'd ever known…or would likely ever know. The only flaw was that she knew that someday it had to end.

"What are you thinking about?" Pan asked.

Nothing she could tell him about but fortunately she had another answer. "I need to go to my apartment this morning. I'm running out of clothes."

He nuzzled her neck, his thin goatee tickling her breasts. "You have clothes here…for when you need to get dressed, which isn't that often." Stretching out on top of her, his legs became a warm blanket against hers. "Stay in my bed and I'll keep you warm, little nymph."

It was tempting to do just as he suggested, but she laughed instead. "I can't stay in bed all day, Pan, and I'm tired of the clothes I have here. Besides there is other stuff I want."

He nipped at her earlobe, giving it a gentle tug with the flat edges of his teeth. "You sleep here with me, but keep your things in an apartment way over in Elysian Fields. Why do you keep your own place? I have room here for your 'stuff'."

She leaned away so she could see his face, her own no doubt showing her astonishment at his suggestion. "Are you suggesting I move in with you? But Pan, we don't know how long this will last!"

Pan sat up, yawned and stretched. "It has lasted long enough for your commuting to your place every few days to become a problem. I merely suggest you move the things you want daily here and keep your apartment for long-term storage. I can make room for your belongings and it would be more efficient."

"Room where?" Nina waved her hands, indicating Pan's bedchamber, which was the only covered portion of his garden home. A set of pegs along one wall held his collection of loincloths, the only clothing he usually wore outside of a couple of shirts and slacks. There were no other storage areas available.

As a romantic bower, Pan's place was great, but it lacked a few amenities when it came to living space. For one thing Nina was using her empty guitar case to store the few clothes she'd brought. The case was what she'd used to smuggle Eros' bow and arrow set into Pan's garden that fateful day, but it had come in handy.

"I just can't see myself living here, Pan," she told him.

"Why not? What does your place have that mine doesn't?"

"Oh, just a few things. Like closets, chests, and a decent bathroom."

Pan glowered at her list of his home's failings. "There is a perfectly fine bathing area in my garden. It has a waterfall, hot and cold water, and a natural fountain."

Nina rolled her eyes. "True, the bathing pool is nice, but it's outside and uncovered. A lady likes a little privacy when she's taking a bubble bath and washing her hair. Anyone flying overhead can watch me in there."

A frown crossed Pan's face, as if he didn't like the idea of someone viewing Nina bathing. "I have noticed Mercury flitting across more than he used to," he mused. "Perhaps a shelter over that corner of the garden would be in order."

He looked around the bower. "If you need storage space, we can make some for you." Stepping over to the corner, he whispered something to the living trees that formed the walls and the roof over their heads. There was a rustling of leaves then the branches seemed to bow in unison.

As Nina watched, buds formed along the inner edges of two trees and tendrils sprouted. They grew and began to wind around each other, forming a basket weave wall.

With a wave of his hand, Pan gestured to the slowly forming wall of new growth. "It will take a little while, but you'll have your closet soon."

"How do you do that?" Nina asked, awed by his powers.

He laughed. "I ask for what I need and the plants serve me. I can teach you to commune with nature and ask it for what you want."

"I couldn't do that…"

"Of course you can. As long as you are here, you might as well learn to care for the garden. That way you'll be more comfortable here."

Not much point in learning Pan's nature-boy ways since any time now he was going to lose interest and send her on her way, but what did she have to lose? Maybe she could get into landscaping if she ever decided to leave the world of adult television. "I'd be happy to learn from you."

Her answer had pleased him. "Excellent. We can get started right away…"

"Not this morning, Pan. I still need to pay a visit to my apartment. And then I have to go to work…"

"Work?" Pan folded his arms and glared at her. "I thought you quit that job of yours."

Nina cringed. She hadn't meant to blurt that out. Pan had been livid when he'd found out she worked at a twenty-four hour adult cable station, sometimes even starring in the productions. He'd read her the riot act about "behavior unbecoming a minor deity", and how no nymph he was living with would go from his bed to have sex with a human on television, even if it was simulated.

"I didn't actually quit. I transferred to production instead." She grinned happily. "I'm a director and they told me I could produce my own script."

The god didn't look happy about the situation. "I'm not sure I want you there at all, even if it is behind the camera."

Nina's heart sank. She'd worked hard to get promoted to production and didn't want to give it up. Once Pan dumped her, working at LUV would be all she had left.

For a moment she considered arguing. After all, he couldn't really tell her what to do, but then inspiration struck. "Maybe you could help me with the script. I haven't done that much writing before."

"You'd want Homer or Apollo for that. I'm not much of a writer."

"But you know do how to describe sex acts and are always coming up with little skits. You do it all the time when we're together. You know, like when we play 'the naughty little lamb' or 'the shepherdess and the big, bad goat'."

Pan grinned. "I've always liked being the big, bad goat." He advanced on her, the front of his loincloth rising.

Nina backed away. Not that she would really say no, but she did have to get moving if she were to get to work on time. "I'm sure lots of other people would enjoy it too. You could help me write some of your skits into a script."

"It could be an interesting thing to do. I've always wanted to do more in the arts." Pan stroked his beard. "Very well. I'll help you with your script as long as you don't act it out with anyone else...besides me, of course. I have your promise?"

As if it would be *her* cheating on *him*! Grimly Nina beat down her inner vengeance nymph, who wanted to protest that aloud. She'd brought up Pan's indiscretion a couple times in the past five months but he'd always claimed he couldn't remember the incident...stating that since it hadn't made that much of an impression on him, it shouldn't be a factor now.

Instead she nodded, putting her most virtuous look on her face. It was the one she'd used at the beginning of the film *The Naughty Nun*, when she'd played Sister Lovesalot. "I promise, Pan. No fooling around."

"Good. One more thing. I want you to move in here." He glanced back at the walls of the new "closet", which were now four inches long. Their intention seemed to be to block off the corner and make a good-sized storage space. "Your cabinet should be done by tomorrow so I'll help you move your belongings then."

Nina nodded her agreement. At least she was keeping her job, and with Pan's help, she'd have a terrific script to direct. She didn't really mind living with him—only the likely temporariness of it bothered her.

Not that she'd tell him that. Pan didn't need to know that she was really in love with him. It would be the last thing he'd want.

Chapter Two

Pan sighed. Once more he'd awoken with a lovely woman in his bed, holding her close. Not that waking with a woman in his bed was extraordinary. Pan had never been one to sleep alone if he could help it.

And the cuddling wasn't all that unusual either. It wasn't a big secret that Pan enjoyed the feel of a woman next to him nearly as much as he did the actual intimate possession of her.

What was unusual was that the woman he woke with this morning was the same woman he'd woken with yesterday and the day before, the same woman he'd slept with for the past five months since being struck by Eros' arrow. Up to then he'd been happy to have variety in his life, a different woman every night.

Now he rather liked the comfort of the same woman's arms, night after night, as long as the woman was his own Nemesis, or Nina, as she preferred to be called.

Not for the first time, he wondered how this had come to pass. Yes, it was part of the spell on Eros' arrow, but surely that wasn't the only reason. He also wondered why he didn't mind as much as he would have expected to. He should have expected to feel trapped and bored with having the same woman all time. Instead it was actually rather pleasant knowing a woman so intimately that you could anticipate her next breath.

What he didn't like was the instability of their situation. Because of the spell he couldn't anticipate was when she was likely to fall out of love with him. At any time, Nina could decide to leave and that wasn't something he was prepared for.

Pan leaving a woman...that was to be expected. He was comfortable with no longer feeling desire for someone, or finding another woman more attractive. But for a woman to leave him before he was ready for her to go? No...Pan didn't think that was desirable at all.

For the first time, Pan wanted to know how to manage a long-term relationship and keep his woman from leaving. With this in mind, he'd invited one of his best friends to lunch to discuss the matter.

The lunchtime crowd filled the small delicatessen, forcing the gods to sit on the tall stools at the counter. Not that they minded. It was kind of fun to rub elbows with the normal patrons of the place instead of being isolated in a booth. Given the circumstances, Pan had modified his appearance to appear completely human and had even foregone his usual loincloth attire and worn casual khaki pants with a lime green polo shirt, so he fit in with the human crowd around him.

Only if you looked close would anyone notice that the fabric had an unnatural sheen to it and that the shirt's logo was a flying horse. The pants and shirt were from Athena's Spring sportswear collection, the goddess of wisdom having had the foresight to get into the Olympian fashion business when mixing with humans had become easier due to the trans-dimensional transfer system.

While still acceptable casual wear on Olympus, togas were out of style on Earth. The sign on the restaurant wall read "No shoes, no shirt, no service".

Pan liked to think that it dated back to the last time he'd gotten a craving for a good egg-salad sandwich in the middle of the night, but had forgotten to change, and had shown up in the street outside in a loincloth. His appearance had collected quite a crowd, not to mention a large padded van and several burly men in long white coats. He'd transferred back before things got out of hand, but his dignity had taken a beating.

Today no one would look twice at him, although his huge companion caught some folks' attention. So what if the other god was nearly seven feet tall with muscles to rival a movie-star action hero? The way they'd stared, you'd think no one had seen a divine blacksmith before.

Pan finished his grilled cheese sandwich and took a big slug of beer. "What do women want, Hep?"

Hephaestus paused in the middle of his corned beef on rye. "Why ask me, Pan? I'm an ugly, lame guy married to the goddess of love. The most beautiful woman ever created and she's stuck with me, yet she's never made any moves to be quit of our marriage." He took another bite and chewed it carefully. "Hades if I know what women want. You've far more experience with them than I do."

Perhaps Hep was right, but none of his casual experience with women was doing him any good. After Nina had left that morning, Pan had puttered about his garden, encouraging the trees near the bathing pool to start growing a canopy and spending a little more time directing the construction of her closet. It was shaping up nicely and he'd even begun work on a set of drawers for that blasted underwear she continued to use.

Knowing that Nina wouldn't be back until evening, he'd sent a message to Hep, inviting him to lunch at their favorite Los Angeles deli. Not as authentic as the New

York equivalent, but they did have a good selection of vegetarian fare, something that, as a non-meat eater, Pan appreciated.

He wasn't sure why he was asking Hep about this, except that they were friends. Hep was one of the few gods who didn't look down on him for having a body outside of the perfect norm. Having been born ugly and lame to boot, Hephaestus had suffered through plenty of ostracizing as a youth, particularly from his mother, Hera. The head goddess hadn't been the least bit happy to have an ugly child.

He'd been picked on most of his life until he'd grown strong enough to handle the great hammer he used to forge the weapons that made Zeus and the other gods so powerful. Now no one messed with him. Hep had grown into his strength and with his bulging biceps and massive chest he looked powerful enough to break anyone who crossed his path with ease.

But Pan knew that Hep was actually one of the gentlest men around who wouldn't dream of hurting a soul. That was another reason Pan liked the big god, for his even bigger heart. Hep would give him good advice.

Besides, the lame god was in one of the longest lasting marriages with one of the most demanding women on Olympus. He had to be doing something right.

"I've had experience, Hep, but not the right kind. Sure a few more women have been through my bed…" He paused as Hephaestus choked on his sandwich then waited while the gods' weaponsmith took a gulp of beer to clear his throat.

Once the big man could breathe freely again, he glared at Pan. "A few women? Come on, do I look stupid?"

Pan sighed. "All right. I've had a lot of women in my bed..." Under Hep's steady gaze, he added, "and a lot of other places. But the fact remains that relationships are new to me. I'm not used to having a woman...the same woman...around all the time."

Hep resumed eating his sandwich, in smaller bites this time. Pan decided that he didn't want to risk choking again. "So what do you want from me? What kind of relationship do you have with Nina?"

Sexual...but Hep knew that. Pan had even confided in the god of forges about the arrow that had pieced his heart and Nina's, binding them together—temporarily. The problem was that Pan wanted it to be more than that. He didn't want Nina in his bed just because of a bespelled arrow.

"I want her to be happy with me. We're stuck together until the spell wears off and so far she's reluctant to make any plans for the future. It's driving me crazy. I don't even know if she'll speak to me in the morning."

"Does she speak to you?" Hep asked with a devilish grin.

"Well, maybe we don't talk that much," Pan admitted.

Hep chortled. "I could talk to Eros and find out about the spell on the arrow. Maybe it would help to find out what the duration is."

Pan shook his head. "No, better not. Nina stole that bow and the arrow and I don't want her to get into trouble."

"She meant well, didn't she?"

"Yeah. She wanted to help her sister Echo win a man's love." Pan grimaced. "I was trying to seduce Echo at the time. I can't imagine what I was thinking. Nina is so much more my type. We get along great."

He said the last with so much satisfaction that Hep again paused in eating his sandwich to stare at him. His lips twitched in secret mirth. "If you get along so good, why is there a problem?"

"I want more than what we have. Yes, we're great in bed, but I want it to be more than just fucking our brains out. I want to be able to talk to her as well. Make her see we have more in common than sex."

"So you want to have more to talk to her about." Hep shrugged. "What have you tried to do with her so far?"

"I thought I could teach her how to take care of my garden. That way she can make changes when she likes."

"Good. Women like to have a say in their home. I always thought your place could use a woman's touch. A few more comforts...like furniture and pillows. All that wicker seating is hard on a man's rear. And there's other things...stuff that women like to have around."

Like a roof over the bathing pool, Pan acknowledged silently, as well a place to store her clothing and other things. He really had been a bachelor for a long time. He hadn't realized that the secret to making Nina want to be in his home was to make it hers as well. He nodded silently. This was good advice.

"Have you been to her place, seen how it's decorated?"

"Not yet. I plan on going with her tomorrow. I want her to move in with me so I offered to help her move her things."

Hep's grin nearly split his face. "Sounds good. Take a good look around while you're there. You can learn a lot about a woman from the way she keeps her house."

Pan nodded. He'd do just that. "I'd also like to have more in common with her."

"Is there anything that she's interested in?"

Pan thought for a moment and remembered Nina's sudden enthusiasm at becoming a director. "There is her job…"

Hep's bushy eyebrows went up. "She works? I didn't know that."

"She's…in the entertainment business. Has a new job as a director…of short movies." Pan balked at telling his friend what kind of films Nina was involved with. "She asked me to help her with a script and I said I would."

The smith clapped Pan on the shoulder with his massive hand, nearly knocking him off the stool in his enthusiasm. "Why that's just the thing! Help the little lady with her project. She'll be grateful and you'll have something to talk to her about." The big man's eyes lit up. "Hey, you might even get her a present. Something she could use in her writing."

Recovering his seat, Pan returned the big man's grin. "Great advice, Hep. I'll do just that. Look if there is anything I can do for you…"

The smith just shrugged his shoulders. "Things with me and Appie are okay, at least at the moment. I'll keep it in mind though."

Pan suppressed a chuckle. Hep had taken to calling Aphrodite "Appie" some time ago. The goddess had fumed over the nickname until her husband had added to it and called her "Appie-pie" after his favorite dessert.

She'd told him to never call her that again and hadn't complained further about the less repellant nickname.

They finished up lunch and Pan happily paid the bill. For the first time since that blasted arrow had stuck him he felt like he was gaining some control over the situation. It was terrible wondering each day if this would be the last he'd have to hold close his little spitfire of a nymph.

He'd try and get her to fit more into his life and participate more in hers. Even if the spell wore off and Nina stopped being infatuated with him tomorrow, he was at least going to try and keep her around a little longer. He'd found he liked waking up to a single woman in his bed every morning.

No, it was more than that. There was something about the dark-haired minx that appealed to him, beyond what he'd expected from the arrow. He was beginning to suspect that sometime in the past five months he'd really fallen in love with Nina. Unfortunately she didn't love him, really. If she did, she wouldn't keep bringing up the past.

Pan grimaced. Three hundred years ago he'd had a brief affair with Nemesis…brief because she'd ended it when he'd stayed out all night—apparently with another woman. It was scarcely his fault. She hadn't gone to a party with him and he'd gotten a little drunk. The woman had been incidental, but try telling a vengeance nymph that. If only he could remember what happened as well as Nemesis did. The woman had a memory like Mnemosyne, she never forgot and would never really forgive. The only reason she was with him now was the arrow's spell.

The only trouble was convincing her to stay once she no longer was under the spell's influence. He had to prove himself to her. So far sex hadn't done the job. Hopefully Hep's advice would make the difference.

* * * * *

Nina looked up from her new miniature laptop with the upside-down pomegranate on the cover. She stroked the glossy peach-colored surface. "I still can't believe you had Hep make this for me," she told Pan, her voice rich in gratitude.

Pan leaned across the wicker table in the dining area of the garden. "Hey, if you're going to be a writer, you need the tools. A computer to write on is nearly essential these days."

Cautiously she checked the ports in the back. "Will it work on Earth as well as here?"

"Yep. I made sure it would connect using standard human WI-FI wireless networking as well as MOEN." The latter had taken a bit of doing. Pan and Hep had needed to involve Mercury, the expert in Mount Olympus Ethereal Networking, to get the specifications Hep needed for the cross-network mapping module. It had taken some effort but they'd finally worked out the bugs in the system.

The smith had been very pleased with the result and had discussed patenting the computer and its underlying technologies, including Mercury on the project of course. They'd even brainstormed a marketing strategy, getting Homer to vet the machine as a writing tool.

"The power converter will switch between human and pantheon current as well. Up here you won't have to worry about battery life, but on Earth you can just plug it into the wall." Pan took it from her and pointed to a small button on the side. "And look, if you touch this, it folds up to fit in your pocket." He demonstrated that feature, then returned it to full size and returned it to her.

Nina threw her arms around the god's neck. "It's beautiful and I love it." She kissed him over and over. "Thank you so much. I wish I had something to give you. Or do I?" she asked, her voice husky.

She felt good in his arms, but Pan knew this wouldn't lead anywhere but to the bedroom. Not that he had anything against that, but this wasn't the time. After all, he wanted her to see they had more in common than just sex.

Pan returned her to her chair and placed her firmly on the seat before returning to his own. With effort, he ignored the bulge in his loincloth that Nina's kisses had provoked. Getting started on this writing project should be what they were focusing on, not his erection.

Or her kisses, no matter how sweet they were.

He tapped the laptop. "Now that you have something to write with, you should get your screenplay started. What kind of story did you have in mind?"

Confusion colored her expression as she reopened the machine and brought up an empty text editor. Pan realized that he'd never turned down one of her advances before. Well, he thought in some satisfaction, maybe now she'd see him as more than just a sex object.

She nibbled her lower lip. "I was seeing it as a series of short sexual scenes held together by a framework. That way it could be viewed as a whole, or just the individual scenes could be used. Sometimes we need filler material of no more than five minutes to put between regular programs and this would give the film more flexibility."

Pan nodded approvingly, a little surprised at how clever this was. He knew Nina was intelligent, but this was savvier than he'd expected. He eyed his little nymph with respect. "So for example, if you were to do some erotic tales of the gods, you could have a bard who is telling the stories to a king as a common link and make a full movie. Later, if you need something shorter, an individual tale would work as well. Good idea."

A deep blush crossed her cheeks as his praise. "I wouldn't do tales of the gods, because they might disapprove of my using their stories that way. But I did have something like that in mind, a storyteller and her stories."

Her words were quick and enthusiastic. Fascinated by this unseen side of a woman he thought he knew so well, Pan leaned towards her. "What storyteller did you have in mind?"

Nina grinned at him. "Did you ever hear of a woman called Scheherazade?" She proceeded to tell him the story of *A Thousand and One Arabian Nights*.

Ten minutes later, Pan stared at her indignantly. "The sultan's wife had to tell him stories to delay her execution?" he said, his voice showing disgust at this twist to the tale. He crossed his long fleece-covered legs in front of him. "And they talk about someone like me being barbaric."

"It was a long time ago," Nina said soothingly. "And she did keep his interest so he didn't fulfill his vow to kill his bride every morning. She was a heroine who saved the women of her kingdom and restored the sanity of the sultan."

"I guess that is one way to look at it. She was certainly a woman to be admired. So how would you envision this story beginning?"

Folding her hands over the keyboard, Nina thought for a moment. "I guess," she said slowly, "I'd see it starting with the sultan and Scheherazade on their wedding night. He'd be having sex with her…"

"Not making love?" Pan interjected.

Nina shook her head emphatically. "They wouldn't love each other. Maybe she'd be in love with him, but the sultan would see her only as something to fuck. He couldn't see her even as a human being at this point…otherwise how could he justify having her killed the next morning? It would be too hard if he actually cared for her. Besides that, he doesn't trust her. The whole reason for his behavior is that he has no faith that a woman won't betray him."

"This is because his former wife made love to another man?" Pan shook his head in dismay. "It is the nature of people to seek variety in their lovers."

Nina went very still. "True," she said slowly, not meeting his gaze. "But few humans cope well with it. They consider it a betrayal when their lover seeks another."

Oops, dangerous territory. Pan tried to laugh if off. "Even so, you'd think a man wouldn't blame all women for the actions of one. He could have even forgiven his wife if she was truly sorry."

"Kind of hard to forgive her after he'd removed her head. But as to the rest, that's what this story is all about…a woman teaching a man how to forgive." Nina replied.

Or a woman learning how to forgive. This could be useful, he thought before returning to the script. "So you start with the sultan having sex with Scheherazade, except he's taking her hard, not caring about her pleasure. It isn't lovemaking."

A thought occurred to him, about when he'd snatched up Nina after being hit with Eros' arrow. He'd been angry at how helpless he'd felt, and had taken some of it out on Nina, forcing her to her knees in front of him. She hadn't seemed to mind at the time.

Still, he thought he understood the sultan a little. "He's angry because he knows he can't love her, otherwise he won't be able to keep his vow. So he's forceful, doesn't try to give her pleasure but takes his own."

The sound of a keyboard intruded on his thoughts—Nina typing away. "That's good," she told him. "Great insight into his character."

"We need to redeem him by the end. Make him understand that he doesn't need to be this way. He needs to trust her."

Nina looked up from her laptop and beamed at him, her smile incandescent. "That would be consistent with the story. We can work in several scenes between them, each a little more loving. Maybe we can have something happen that threatens her and makes the Sultan understand how much she means to him. We should also show that she would never betray him and have him believe it. The last love scene would be them truly making love."

Happy that she liked his idea, Pan watched as she took notes, feeling her enthusiasm rise. He thought about how the ancient storyteller saved her life and won the Sultan's respect and trust.

"So, they finish having sex and he's about to go to sleep when she begins a story that she can't finish before dawn." Pan stared at Nina. "What were her stories about?"

"Oh, she spoke of many tales from the Middle East. Stories about spells, sailors, wizards, and adventures involving magic lamps." Nina thought for a moment. "Djinn showed up sometimes."

Pan grinned. "A sexual story about a Djinn? That could be interesting."

"There was one where a Djinn had been stuck in a bottle for several centuries. When a fisherman freed him, the Djinn threatened to kill him, but he tricked him into rewarding him instead." Nina thought for a moment. "I'm not sure how to make that a sex story."

Pan's grin widened. "The Djinn are very sexual beings. Deprive them of sex for long enough and they get irritable. Suppose it was a woman who opened the bottle. The Djinn threatens to kill her, but she offers to have sex with him and gets him to love her instead."

Nina's eyes went wide. "That's wonderful!" She returned to her machine and her open file. She stared at the blank page.

"So we open on a beach and the woman has just opened the bottle. The Djinn is there, and he's twenty times bigger than she is. He's fuming about being in the bottle so long and threatening to kill her."

"Wait a minute." Pan sat on the table and crossed his legs, doing his best to emulate the stance of an ancient storyteller. "If we're going to do this, let's do it right. I'll dictate and you write."

Clearing his throat, he spoke in the singsong voice of a bard.

"Once a long time ago in a far away land, there was a young fisherwoman named Mirmana, who was poor, but beautiful and very wise. While walking the beach one morning she found a bottle, which seemed very heavy for its size. Curious as to what it contained, she opened it only to discover that it held a Djinn who rose above her in a dark cloud of blue smoke to the size of twenty men.

"The huge creature glared down at her. 'You have freed me, but at the cost of your life. At one time I intended to reward my rescuer, but since then I've grown weary of captivity and will allow no one to have dominance over me. Therefore I have vowed that you must die.'

"The fisherwoman threw herself on the sand and begged the Djinn for her life knowing her pleas were in vain. But as she was on her knees, her cap fell off, revealing her long hair.

"The Djinn stared in surprise. 'A woman? I never expected a woman.' He was perturbed by this turn of events, bothered that his vow meant he would have to slay a woman, something foreign to his nature. To make things worse, his body recognized her attractiveness, and while Mirmara watched, his loincloth lifted before him.

"She swallowed hard at the sight and was overcome with desire herself, even though she was still a maiden. 'Mighty Djinn, before you kill me, I would beg to see that organ of yours, for truly it must be a magnificent sight.'

"The Djinn preened at her praise for he was very proud of his cock. He wasted no time in whipping off his loincloth and revealing himself to her. Indeed his organ was magnificent, taller than the tallest man and round like a tower. If he were to lie on the sand, it would be large enough to shelter her on a rainy night. Mirmara stared and under her admiring gaze, he grew even more erect and knelt on the ground so she could see it closer.

"Growing bold, Mirmara approached him and touched it lightly with her hand. 'It is wondrous indeed, master Djinn. Never have I seen its like.'

"The Djinn purred under her gentle stroke. 'It has been a long time since it has seen relief, little fisherwoman.' He struggled for a moment as if uncertain as to how to request what he wanted. Finally he told her, 'I would spare your life if you would pleasure me.'

"Mirmara shrugged and looked at him sadly. 'I would love to do your bidding, mighty Djinn, and not just to save my life, for I find you fascinating. But while I'm innocent in such things, even I know that something the size of your organ would be difficult for me to pleasure properly. I can't even put my arms around it. Perhaps if you were a bit smaller…' she suggested.

"'Done!' the Djinn cried, and he immediately shrunk to half his height. Now his erection was only the size of a child and easy for Mirmara to take into her arms. She hugged his cock and stroked it, murmuring all the time at how lovely it was. Soon its end was weeping huge drops that splashed as they hit the sand.

"The Djinn groaned under her ministrations. 'That feels so good, little woman. You have won your life from me. I would give you gold if you were to kiss it and lick the tip.'

"Mirmara gazed at him in reproach. 'I would not do such a thing for gold, for I am not a harlot that can be bought. If you enjoy what I do, I would have you give me another reward.'

"'But,' she continued, 'I'm afraid it is still impossible, for even now you are so large that you would barely feel my kisses. Perhaps if you were a bit smaller…'

"'Done!' the Djinn cried again, and shrunk this time to merely twice the size of a normal man. Now his organ was small enough for her to kiss and lick, if not enough for her to take it into her mouth. Still, Mirmara did her best and the Djinn moaned aloud as she caressed his erection with her hands, licking the thick droplets that gathered at its end.

"Now that he was closer to her size, the Djinn could see how infinitely desirable Mirmara was. He looked at her simple fisher garments and with insistent fingers pulled them off her, leaving her as naked as he was. Mirmara blushed as he stripped her, but did not stop him as he bared her heavy coral-tipped breasts and wide hips.

"When the Djinn saw her beauty, he nearly wept with joy. 'You are so lovely, little woman. I wish to worship your body as you have mine.' He pulled her closer and with long thick fingers explored her most secret places, probing them and making her weak with want for him. He drew each of her breasts within his mouth and his tongue lapped her nipples.

"The Djinn gazed at her, his eyes hot with need. 'I would give you anything you wanted, little woman, if you let me have your body to satisfy my desire.'

"Mirmara wanted the Djinn as well, but was still afraid. 'I would give myself willingly, mighty Djinn, for you are the comeliest man I've ever known, and have the most talented fingers and tongue. But I fear you are still too large. I am an innocent and you would kill me with your organ.'

"The Djinn smiled at her and shrank one last time until he was the size of an ordinary man. He held her close in his arms and kissed her lips gently. 'I would have you know only my desire, sweet maiden, and not fear at my touch.'

"Lowering Mirmara to the sand, the Djinn covered her with his body. One swift thrust and he took her maidenhead with his cock, filling her completely. Mirmara cried out at the small pain, but then moaned as he pulled back before entering her again. He set a rhythm and soon they moved in that sensuous dance of lovers, the Djinn taking pleasure in Mirmara's sweetness.

"They made love for some time, but not nearly long enough for the Djinn's mind. He had been too long in the bottle and came quickly, but he made certain that Mirmara reached ecstasy with him.

"As they lay together on the sand, the Djinn wondered what reward to give this no- longer-maid, since she did not want gold or other riches. Finally he asked her name.

"'I am called Mirmara, mighty Djinn.'

"The Djinn laughed. 'A lovely name, and suitable for a Djinn's wife. I would have you wed to me if that reward pleases you, sweet Mirmara, for you have earned my love and erased the hate from my mind.'

"Mirmara smiled. 'Your reward pleases me, lord…but only under one condition.'

"The Djinn gazed at his soon to be bride in surprise. 'And what condition would that be, lovely Mirmara?'

"'Well, my lord.' Mirmara said with a blush, 'the next time you shrink to make love with me…could you stay a little bit larger?'"

Pan finished the story with a smirk and Nina laughed loudly, still typing the story in as fast as she could.

"That is wonderful, Pan!" she said. "Funny and sexy at the same time."

He laughed. "And there is a lesson, as well."

Nina's hands paused over the keyboard. "There is?"

"The Djinn intended to kill the person who opened the bottle but changed his mind after knowing more about her. The lesson is that you shouldn't be too sure of what you want until you know what you are dealing with and that a man shouldn't be afraid to change his mind."

Nina finished typing and saved the file. "That would be what Scheherazade tells the sultan. Like the Djinn he'd planned on killing her but learned to love his rescuer instead." She closed her laptop and carried it to their bedroom.

Pan gazed after her and spoke quietly to himself. "It could be a lesson for both of us, little nymph. Like the Djinn, I was not sure of what I wanted...but I am now."

Chapter Three

Morning again came to Mount Olympus and Nina awoke in Pan's embrace, his deep slow breathing telling her that he still slept. She snuggled deeper into his arms, reveling in his unconsciously tight hold on her. So warm, so loving. If she didn't know it to be arrow-influenced, she'd almost suspect he really wanted to embrace her this way, as if she were the only woman in the pantheon for him.

From where she lay she could see the mixture of tree branches and vines that formed her new closet. It had completed its growth yesterday and all she had to do now was pack what she wanted from her apartment and move it here. She had to admit she was surprised that Pan had insisted she move in with him. To the best of her knowledge, he'd never had a roommate before.

Maybe he was as tired of the uncertainty in their situation as she was. If so, she'd have expected him to want her gone, but instead he seemed to want to make their relationship more permanent.

She wasn't sure how to take this from him. Other than to be delighted it was happening, that is. And to hope his desire for her as a roommate lasted longer than it took for her to unpack her things.

Last night they'd worked on her script on her new laptop and she'd gotten part of her framework and the first tale of her Arabian nights. After he'd dictated it once, she'd asked him to do it again, this time with them acting out the parts of the horny Djinn and innocent Mirmara.

Nina grinned. Pan really knew how to act. She couldn't wait to tackle their next project. Maybe Sinbad and the Wicked Mermaid?

Behind her a long sensuous finger caressed her backbone and Nina startled at the touch. Now she noticed how Pan's breathing picked up as he pressed harder into her back. His cock grew along the cleft of her ass, hardening to readiness.

Pan was awake and apparently interested in action. Nina pressed back into him, letting him know without words she too was awake. Sometimes they did it this way, using actions to signal what they desired rather than speaking aloud. It was fun playing games with Pan, and after all, actions often spoke louder than words.

His wayward finger continued to explore, sliding down her spine until it found the slit between her ass-cheeks. With a single stroke it located her anus, prodding the puckered opening with obvious intent.

Nina's heartbeat picked up. Ah…that kind of action. Well, it had been a while since they'd played that game. Several hundred years in fact, but that's what she loved about Pan. He was always ready for anything sensual even if it was a little out of the ordinary.

She lifted her ass a little, giving him better access to her. That might have been enough, but when he didn't immediately take advantage, she decided to break the unspoken no-speaking rule.

"In the mood for something different this morning?" she asked.

"That depends...are you interested?" Pan's voice still showed its early morning huskiness, but there was something else as well. Nina wondered when she'd last heard such uncertainty in a man's voice.

She could have laughed aloud at that unlikelihood. Imagine Pan feeling uncertain about anything. Besides, with him she was interested in anything and she didn't have any real problems with this kind of game. "I'm interested, Pan. Do we have what we need?"

Gods didn't need condoms, but Nina insisted on a certain amount of lubricant. Sex involving pain had never been that high on her list of sensual interests.

Pan hadn't ever expressed an interest in S&M, either. For him, she might reconsider, but part of her was glad he wasn't attracted to that kind of game.

Of course she was just glad he was in bed with her every morning.

Turning from her, Pan fumbled in the living wicker basket that filled the role of a bedside table. Nina watched as he pulled forth a tube with a familiar label. She grinned. It was a brand she was fond of as well, water-based with a mild flavor that didn't overpower the natural taste of a lover. She and Pan really did have similar tastes.

"That will do nicely," she told him.

Turning onto her knees, she tried to relax as he coated her opening with the lube, using his fingers to tease her open. She moaned, particularly when he used his other hand to play with her clit and pussy. In moments her body was hot and heavy and she was desperate with need. Need for him, for his cock, somewhere...anywhere.

The hand playing with her anus disappeared. Nina looked back to see Pan smearing lube on his cock, coating it thickly. He closed his eyes and smiled as he stroked his shaft, perhaps remembering another's hand doing the same thing, caressing his cock.

Someone other than her, perhaps? Nina's enthusiasm dampened a little at the thought of a now-past rival for Pan's affections. But when he opened his eyes to gaze into hers, she felt the weight of his desire for her all over again and her pulse raced. She was the woman Pan was with now and that was all that mattered.

He seized her hips and seated himself against her, his voice husky with need. "Stop me if this hurts."

As if she'd ever stop him, no matter what. Still, it was nice of him to say it. Thrusting forward, he entered her with just the tip of his cock, slowly teasing the tiny hole open. At each miniscule stroke, he paused to let her adjust to his bulk. For once Nina wasn't thrilled with his massive size. It did hurt, a little, but she quickly dismissed that as he reached forward and his hand drove her clit into a full orgasm. She cried out, jerking back against him, and when she finished Pan was fully embedded inside her.

Oh, now that was clever. Bring a lover to orgasm and impale her while she wasn't paying attention. He hadn't done that before. Pan had learned some new tricks in the years they hadn't been together.

The many, many years. That thought should have bothered her, but for now it was enough that it was her back Pan leaned against and that he was embedded deep within her ass. She could live without knowing from whom he'd learned this trick or the names of those he'd practiced it with. For the moment Pan was her lover, and that was all that mattered.

She leaned forward onto her elbows, giving him control. In this position Pan controlled their coupling with Nina submissive to him. Not normally her favorite position but as he took first one stroke then another, she gave up worrying over who was on top. All that mattered was how wonderful being fucked by him was, in any position, in any act imaginable. Pan was her lover and he could take her anyway he wanted.

He took it slow and easy on her. This wasn't a harsh buggering that would leave her raw and aching but something else. Pan showed care for her, more than she'd expected. She'd never been all that excited by anal intercourse, but this time, with him, it was still lovemaking as far as she was concerned.

As far as he was concerned as well, she realized. Pan may have held another this way, used their body for his needs, but she wondered if he'd caressed their hips as he did hers, or fondled their clit with such loving care. Or cock, for that matter. Pan had occasionally taken male lovers to satisfy his sexually adventuresome nature.

Maybe he had fondled others the way he did her, but for the moment Pan was neither heterosexual nor homosexual but purely Nina-sexual. He was her lover and no other's.

For the moment. Who knows how long that would last? But Nina wasn't going to worry about that now. She was having sex with the man she loved.

Pan sped up and she pushed her clit more into his hand, her breath nearly frantic as his fingers drove her closer to ecstasy. Her orgasm came hard and she bucked against him. The ring of her ass tightened around him, and a hiss of near pain came from behind her.

Pan dropped onto her back and threw his arms around her waist, hugging her close into his chest. Draped on top of her, he groaned, his body tightening and then she felt the hot blast of his cum shoot deep inside her. He collapsed for a moment, his heart pounding against her back, in odd synchronicity with her own pulse. Shaken to her core, Nina reveled in their closeness, too overcome for speech.

She almost whimpered when Pan slid out of her and drew her closer into his arms and held her, his breath hot against her cheek. Deep shudders still ran through him, aftermaths of his climax. Nina leaned into him, still short of breath herself.

One hand idly stroked her cheek, the caress tender. He chuckled. "I guess I don't need to ask if you want to be with me this morning."

"No, you don't," she agreed, snuggling closer into his chest.

"Good. That's one less thing to do in the morning."

Lifting her head, Nina noted the smile in his face, and she detected more than a little satisfaction in his reply. Was Pan becoming so sure of her presence in his life as to want to skip their ritual morning greeting? Surely that wasn't a good thing.

Or was it? It might mean that he was recognizing her place with him and that he no longer needed to question her continual presence. He could be becoming content with their relationship. In fact, he might even have grown happy with it.

Would an arrow spell have this effect after all this time? Nina wondered at that. Pan was acting like a…a…*husband* might act!

Nina opened her mouth to talk to him about it, but with a final kiss on her forehead he pulled away from her and exited the bed. She watched as he pulled another of his loincloths off a peg and dressed.

She really had to do something about his sense of style. A man should wear something besides a piece of fabric wrapped around his waist, no matter how well it suited his physique. After all, she knew fashion…he should stay somewhat in step with her.

Finished assembling his minimalist clothing, Pan turned his amused gaze on her. "So are you going to stay in bed all day, lazybones? We need to get to your place to pack." With that comment he bounced out of the bower, probably headed for the garden's rudimentary kitchen to prepare breakfast.

Reaching for her simplistic Olympian gown, Nina grumbled to herself. Oh goody. More lightly sweetened granola with milk and herbal tea with a few grapes for dessert.

Yum, yum. She'd lost a few pounds since living with Pan, and for more reasons than having an active sex life. Pan's cooking had its limitations and it showed in their diet.

Maybe she could talk to her sister Chloe and get some pointers on cooking. She bet Pan would love some of Chloe's home-baked breakfast cake. Fastening the shoulder clips of her gown, she headed for the doorway. "Yeah, breakfast cake. That plus a really good espresso machine, that's what we need."

* * * * *

So this was Nina's home. With curious eyes Pan looked around the living room/bedroom of the small studio apartment. It was identical to the many other apartments in this building, one of the many identical dwellings in Elysian Fields, Olympus' answer to affordable housing. This was where most of the minor Olympians lived when they weren't doing their jobs on Earth.

Hep had said he might learn something about Nina through her belongings, so Pan took careful note of his surroundings.

One thing he'd learned already—she sure liked the color red. And black. Everywhere he looked was those colors. There were red and black fabrics, black furniture, and wall and window coverings in the same solemn tones.

Pan frowned. It was rather dismal as a color scheme. Moreover, it didn't really seem like Nina, at least not the Nina he knew. Or thought he knew.

Sure she'd worn a lot of black in the past and even when she'd first come to live with him, much of her clothing had been that way. But in the past few months, the whole palette of her clothing had gotten lighter. The gown she wore today was even a pastel pink, something new that she'd picked up recently.

Maybe her tastes had changed? If so, it was for the better.

Nina came in from what she'd described as her kitchen, hauling a complicated piece of equipment with metal tubes and glass carafes. She beamed at him. "I knew I had this in there somewhere!"

After eyeing the apparatus uneasily, Pan took it from her and placed it on the tall pile of belongings they'd already accumulated. "What is it?" he asked.

"A combination coffee-and-espresso maker. One of the best on the market."

Pan eyed the dust on it. "It doesn't look like it's gotten much use. Why do we need it?"

"Oh, well." Nina said. "I got it a long time ago but never really got the hang of using it." She held up the instruction manual and placed it on the pile. A sheepish look crossed her face. "I've never been that interested in cooking and it was always easier to go out. But now we stay home more and I've been thinking of learning..."

Nina was considering learning to cook? Pan could barely hide his smile. It had to be a good sign when the woman you wanted to live with became interested in domesticity.

Waving his hand, Pan transported the pile, including the coffee-espresso maker, back to his garden. He wasn't all that fond of the distillation of coffee beans, but he'd drink gallons of it if it meant keeping Nina happily at home with him.

Rubbing his hands together, he looked around the apartment. "So, what else do you want?" He lifted the black and red comforter off the queen-sized bed in corner of the room, revealing black satin sheets. "How about these?" he asked.

For an instant, he thought she might actually be blushing. "No, I don't think so. I like your bedding."

Pan had a mental image of Nina's paleness against black satin and his cock hardened in reaction. Oh, yes, the sheets had to come.

"It never hurts to have extras," he told her, pulling them off the bed. As he tugged, a long white shape fell out of the bed from where it had been stuck under the comforter. Curious, Pan picked it up, and noting it was a pillow about the size and shape of a bolster, covered in sheepskin. He held it out to Nina with a questioning look.

She snatched it from his hands, color high in her cheeks and he wondered why. What did Nina have to be self-conscious about?

"It's a pillow..." she told him, not meeting his eyes. "I liked to sleep with it...when I slept alone."

What was so embarrassing about a pillow, he wondered, then inspiration struck. Maybe it was that she sometimes didn't have a bed partner. Pan held up his hands and laughed. "It's all right, Nina. We all sleep alone sometimes and it isn't like it's a teddy bear or something like that. Do you want to bring it with you?"

She placed it back on the bed, rubbing her hand along the surface, a bemused smile on her face. "No, I don't need it. It can stay here," she told him and returned to the kitchen. Pan heard more sounds of metal on metal.

He leaned over to stroke the pillow the way she had. Funny, it reminded him of something, but he couldn't quite place what. Still if Nina didn't want it that was fine with him. He didn't care for animal products like skins in his home.

The bookcase caught his attention. Perhaps there were more clues to what Nina liked in here. Lips twitching with amusement, Pan read the titles and authors. *The Kama Sutra*, a couple of books by Don Juan, several by the Marquis De Sade, and a worn copy of *The Joy of Sex*, complete with bookmarks. On a separate shelf he found an elaborately illustrated version of *One Thousand and One Arabian Nights*, which Pan seized along with the others. Good reference material, he decided, and sent the collection on its way to his bower. He'd have to enlarge the bedroom's bookshelf to hold it all, but one could never have enough good reading material.

Particularly this kind of reading material.

Looking further he found another shelf that held photo albums marked "Dodi Does It…" with the numbers one through ten. Pan opened the first one and nearly dropped it when he noted the subject matter of the photos. Each page was full of still pictures of men and women, mostly naked, having sex in assorted and often imaginative ways.

Very imaginative in some cases. He thought he knew every position possible and some of these he hadn't heard of or would have even thought possible. Still, they were inspirational. His cock got harder than it had when he'd seen the satin sheets.

Pan started to close the book, intending to add it to the reference materials he'd already transported, when he noticed how often a certain dark-haired woman showed up in the pictures. Here she was with a dildo in her hand, stroking it deep inside another woman. Here she had a man's penis in her mouth.

Here she was in a scene not unlike the one he'd had with Nina this morning, except that the hair in the picture was longer and the man sodomizing her wasn't him. Pan pulled another of the albums. Similar pictures, with different people, but always the same woman with dark hair, which was shorter in this album. The third and fourth were the same.

Shaken, Pan replaced the albums on the shelf. Sure, at some level he'd known that Nina was an experienced woman, but he hadn't realized just how experienced she was. Plus to keep photographic evidence of her conquests…at least he hadn't done that.

"What are you looking at?" Nina bounded in from the kitchen with a pile of bowls and utensils in her arms. She plopped her finds on the table and came to join him. Her smile faded as she saw Pan's face and the book in his hand, and the obviously disheveled albums.

"I see you found my pictures," she said, her voice suspiciously even in tone. Perhaps this was another thing she'd been hiding from him?

She took the album from his hands and opened it. "These are stills from my TV series *Dodi Does It Everywhere*. It was very popular, ran for a full ten seasons and went into syndication. I still get hefty residuals from it." She turned the pages, indicting some of the pictures that had appeared in Pan's judgment to be humanly impossible, or even hard for a god to manage.

Her slight smile told him she'd noticed his bemused look. "Many of the poses are staged."

Pan pointed to one of Nina with two men, one entering her from behind while she sucked the cock of the other. "That was staged?"

She laughed but it sounded uncomfortable. "No, not that one," she admitted. Closing the album, she returned it to the shelf then turned to face him. "Pan, you know I used to be in films like that and you've known it for a long time. I fucked a lot of men and women—that was my job and I have to say that I enjoyed it."

At some level he had known and had accepted her past. But it was one thing to know she'd had sex with a lot of other people, it was another to have explicit pictures of it. Besides, she'd been with so many people, and now he was the only man in her life—as far as he knew.

No, he'd know if she was cheating on him. He was a god, after all. But suppose she missed all those other lovers, particularly the women and having her pick of men. Did it satisfy her to only have sex with him?

When he looked at her, Nina's eyes were searching his face, something like desperation in them. "Does my past really bother you, Pan?"

He put on as much of reassuring smile as he could. "Not that much. It was more of a surprise, that's all."

Her smile seemed genuine as she headed for her bathroom to pack her toiletries. "I'm glad you aren't upset. After all, it was in the past and now that I'm directing I don't have sex with the actors anymore."

Pan picked up one of the albums again. "You certainly had a variety of sex in the past. Do you miss it?"

Nina popped her head out of the bathroom doorway. "Do I miss what?"

"The variety…of sex."

"You mean like this morning?" Nina laughed. "Variety is always fun, Pan."

Pan sighed. Sexual variety was great if it didn't mean other lovers. He'd had extras in the bed in the past, but not when he was with someone he cared about. He cared about Nina more than any one he'd ever been with before.

Somehow he just couldn't see adding someone into their lovemaking right now, if ever. He wanted to be Nina's only lover and she was the only woman he wanted. Perhaps because of the past between them she didn't believe that, but it was the truth and someday he'd make her believe it. He didn't want to share her with anyone.

But she liked variety. Pan resisted the urge to groan aloud. Hep had told him he'd find out a lot from her place, but this wasn't something he'd wanted to know.

She emerged from the bathroom with a large cardboard box. Pan stared at it. "How much shampoo do you have?"

"Oh, this isn't just soap, Pan." Nina had a wicked grin on her face. "Just a few items that I think you might enjoy. No peeking, though!" she admonished on handing over the box.

It was heavy and he wondered what was inside, but couldn't steal a look while she was standing there. With a grunt, Pan sent it on its way, along with the last of the kitchen items on the table.

He gathered Nina into his arms. "Are you ready to go?" After a long look around the lonely little apartment, she nestled deep into his arms and nodded her head, sighing into his chest.

"Take me home, Pan."

Chapter Four

Nina was making breakfast. After five months of Pan getting out of bed before her and preparing food in his primitive kitchen, she'd decided it was her turn to cook for him. The time was right. It was the morning after they'd moved her belongings into his garden. Her first official act as lady of the house would be this, making a splendid meal to celebrate her presence.

She had her coffeemaker from her apartment. Pan had fixed up a countertop for it to sit on and a small stove similar to what humans used in the modern world. The simple cold water-based cooler he'd used had been replaced with a refrigerator/freezer. She even had a dishwasher.

Nina had sent a hurried message to her sister Chloe the day before announcing her new living arrangement and seeking guidance. In true Chloe fashion, she'd responded with her heartiest congratulations, a set of shining pots and pans, and a cookbook with some wonderful sounding recipes marked with sticky notes. Eager to try out her new domestic wings, Nina had crept out of Pan's bed before the sun rose, hoping to have an excellent breakfast waiting for him when he finally awakened.

It was all perfect. There was only one hitch.

She had no idea what she was doing.

Nina looked up from the coffeecake page in the cookbook and for the hundredth time that morning wished she'd spent more time actually watching Chloe in the kitchen rather than drinking coffee and talking sex with her. Surely then she'd understand what it meant to separate an egg or sift together the dry ingredients. For a moment she considered teleporting her sister there to help but she didn't have the power to make such a transfer without Pan's help.

Besides, with her luck, she'd get Chloe out of bed and if she were really unlucky, her sister and Alex would have been "occupied". Since the pair had gotten engaged, it seemed like every time she'd called, they'd been sexually busy.

Nina shook her head wryly. And folks thought she and Pan had an active sex life. From the way her sister and her soon-to-be husband went at it, she sometimes thought they could tell her how best to keep a relationship alive.

But sex wasn't what she needed advice on now. What she needed to do was learn to cook. She looked at the barely lightening Olympian sky. It was too early to consult anyone, even if she had known of a great chef on Olympus to talk to.

If only there was some way to find answers without directly asking someone…

Nina's depressed gaze fell on the pomegranate-decorated laptop sitting on her new desk and her mood elevated. Pan had assured her it had wireless networking but she hadn't tried to connect to Earth's internet. Maybe there was hope if she could connect into it. After all she'd heard about this human search engine where it was said you could find anything with just a few well-chosen keywords and a little time.

Moments later, Nina happily cracked an egg over a bowl and, carefully following the directions on the glowing laptop screen, separated the clear white from the yolk. Grinning, she tossed the empty shell into the garbage basket. Thank the gods for technology. With a little help from a search engine she'd found a "cooking for kids" website complete with pictures of common cooking techniques. Satisfaction filled her as she completed adding the ingredients for the coffeecake that Chloe had marked with note reading "Alex's favorite". This was going to be a cinch!

She lost some of her enthusiasm when she pulled the cake pan out of the oven an hour later and examined the contents. The instructions said to stick a toothpick in to check how done it was, but it was clear that the thin twig she'd substituted wasn't going to come cleanly out of the still runny batter.

What could she have done wrong? She'd followed all the instructions. Baffled, she held the pan for a while before realizing she was doing so without any protection from heat. And yet, the pan was barely warm…

With a groan, Nina put it on top of the stove and checked the oven's controls. Sure enough, the temperature gauge was set to the minimum. She rechecked the recipe, only now seeing the small print at the top of the page "preheat oven to 350" and another groan escaped her. No wonder it hadn't cooked.

Turning the knob to the correct temperature, Nina collapsed on a stool to wait. Maybe breakfast could still be saved and if Pan slept in a little longer he'd never know how she'd messed up.

"Good morning," a sexy voice said and a familiar thrill went down her spine. Eyes twinkling, Pan moved around her in the kitchen and examined the cake pan on top of the stove. He gave the contents a skeptical look.

"Hmm, what's for breakfast?"

Nina snatched the pan from him. "It's a surprise. Just needs to cook."

He took a glance at the oven and an amused look crossed his face. Maybe he guessed what she'd done wrong, but if so, he'd decided not to mention it. Wise of him Nina thought, inserting the pan into the now correctly heated oven. She'd have hated to start their first morning of domestic bliss with violence.

Instead, he examined the contents of the carafe in the coffeemaker, which Nina had managed to activate. To her pleasure this was one time where things had worked out right and she'd managed to make actual coffee. Even to her palate the results had been spectacular. Nina held her mug and sipped the rich brew.

Ah. Not even Echo…that is, Chloe, could have done as well.

With a resigned sigh Pan picked up his mug and filled it, then took a tentative sip. From the way he was behaving, she thought he might expect the brew to be laced with hemlock.

An odd expression crossed his face and he took a deeper sip. Narrow eyebrows arched nearly to his tiny horns as surprise took over his face. "That's pretty good!" He spied the sugar on the counter and helped himself to a teaspoon. At her steady stare he shrugged apologetically. "It just needs a little sweetening."

Nina tried not to laugh. For Pan everything had to be a little sweet. Even her. Fortunately it was getting easier for her behave that way for him.

Maybe a little too easy, she thought to herself as he moved to the chairs near their table. Sometimes she wondered if she were still the same nymph she used to be, Nemesis, enemy of all. She couldn't seem to work up a good antipathy against anyone anymore. Particularly not so long as she was around a certain hairy-legged horned-headed god.

Was that such a bad thing, to not be anyone's enemy? Nina sipped her coffee and considered the matter. Perhaps not. There really hadn't been a whole lot of satisfaction in destroying other people's lives. She'd had much more fun as an adult movie star, and did now as a writer and producer. Everyone she knew had adjusted to living in a modern world.

Narcissus had learned to love another person besides himself and was now Nick Rockman, college professor, and happily married to Violet.

Echo, whose claim to fame was being unable to say more than the last words of anyone she met, had fallen in love with Alex, a man incapable of loving her. But then she'd moved into his home, earned his love in spite of everything, and had become a gourmet cook and the owner of a small restaurant chain.

Both of them had grown beyond the limits that history placed on them. Why couldn't she do the same? She could stay with Pan, be his lover and the mistress of his garden home.

A surge of excitement passed through her. Why not? Why couldn't she drop her Nemesis persona and become simply Nina. Nina the writer. Nina the homemaker.

Pan's Nina.

Her gaze fell on him, sipping his now sweetened-to-taste coffee with relish. It was so tempting…to make plans for them, to plan on staying with him for the rest of eternity.

But then reality crashed in on her as she remembered why it was they were together in the first place. It was because of the spell, the one on the arrow that had passed through both of them. Pan loved her only because of that and sometime the spell would fade and he'd no longer want her in his life, just like before. Without the spell keeping him faithful, he'd be checking out the latest nymphs in the forest…or the next vestal virgin looking for a change in her life.

It was inevitable that would happen. Sure, there had been a couple times in the past few months that she'd talked to Pan about his previous defection and he'd told her flat-out he didn't want anyone but her. But how could she possibly trust that? He was still under the arrow's spell, just like she was. What would she do when the day came that he no longer was bound to her? How could she survive if she was no longer Nemesis? Could she go back to her previous nature, particularly if that wasn't really her anymore?

Would enough of her be left after Pan's defection to survive without him? With him, she had no doubts, but without his warming presence could she live on without the edge of animosity to keep her going?

Could she live without hate? She wasn't so sure.

Nina sighed and sipped the now bitter-tasting brew in her cup. She'd have to keep a little of herself in reserve to protect herself. Avoid giving in to him completely, no matter what or she'd be lost when she he left her. No matter what, she'd have to guard her heart, or it would be broken as easily as a ceramic cup.

Pan could become bored with her at any time as the spell began to fade. Even now he could be thinking of ways to keep his interest, or looking for new sport in the game of love. She'd have to keep watch for that. It could signal the end of their relationship.

*****

Later that day in the dark paneled den of his best friend, Pan leaned into the thickly padded back of an armchair and took a good deep sip of his beer. *Ah…sweet with just a hint of bitter, the color of the brew a rich amber, thick head, full-bodied, just the way he liked it.* He raised his glass in a salute to his host.

"Hep, you get better at this every time."

The smith and part-time brewmaster smiled and grabbed his own mug. With a bow he took the seat opposite Pan. "I've been at it for over a thousand years. I should be pretty good at it." He tried his own glass and whistled appreciatively. "Very good, even if I do say so myself."

"Dionysius might have the winemaking for the gods locked up, but you brew the best beer, Hep, no doubt about it. I'll have to make sure that I pick some up to bring home to Nina."

"Yes, the amber is a particular favorite of the ladies. Even my own likes it, and we know Appie enjoys white wine best."

A hint of melancholy covered the big man's face at the mention of his wife, but Pan knew better than to question it. Hep often became gloomy over Aphrodite and their relationship. It was as if he expected that at any time the woman would come to her senses and leave him without warning.

Come to think of it, that wasn't too far off from how Pan thought of Nina. When would his little Nemesis fall out of bespelled love with him?

At least now he had her moved into his home. If she did leave, she'd have to go through a great deal of trouble. Maybe just the thought of hauling her belongings back to her tiny apartment would be too much for her.

Anything to discourage her from leaving…anything to keep her where she belonged…with him!

He had to admit, things were looking up. Nina, never the most domestic nymph around, seemed to be settling in nicely. She'd even cooked him breakfast this morning, which had turned out to be delicious in spite of its rocky start where she'd forgotten to turn on the oven. Keeping Hep's advice in mind about how she should have some say in his place, he'd given her a brief lesson in coaxing his garden to grow the various containers and furnishings she wanted.

Even better, in recent days she hadn't mentioned anything at all about their past. Perhaps it was possible she'd forgiven him.

As of this afternoon she was content. Having unpacked and put away her things, she'd taken her laptop and begun transcribing the notes she'd taken while they had brainstormed her movie, transforming them into screenplay format. As quiet as the machine was, the steady tapping of the keys had gotten on his nerves after a while. After being assured that he wasn't needed for any acting out of sex scenes, something he'd most certainly want to be involved in, he'd sought refuge at Hep's home until dinnertime.

The only issue with visiting the gods' weaponsmith was running into Aphrodite. Every time they'd seen each other during the past several months she'd had trouble keeping a straight face. The goddess of love was obviously pleased with the results of her "little joke", shooting Nina and him with the same arrow and making them fall in love. Pan grinned to himself. What would the goddess think if she realized that he wasn't all that dismayed by her trick anymore?

In fact, he was getting more than a little used to it and was beginning to think he should thank her for intervening. Not that he'd ever tell her that. Aphrodite was arrogant enough without him adding to her reasons for it.

Fortunately for him, it appeared that the goddess was elsewhere this afternoon. Moreover, as he looked around it was clear that she'd been elsewhere for a while. Pan could tell from Hep's disgruntled mood and the miscellaneous glassware and dishes strewn about the place. While the smith was diligent in keeping his forge and work areas neat, his home quickly degenerated when his wife was gone. From the clutter Pan estimated that Aphrodite must have been gone for at least a couple of days.

"How is the little writer doing, Pan?" Hep broke in on his musings. "Making any progress?"

Pan smiled. "Actually, yes. Between the computer and my help, she's almost done with her first scene. She's doing a screenplay based on Scheherazade's Arabian nights."

"Is she?" Hep seemed pleased. "An excellent choice of subject. Lots of opportunities to get creative." He grinned knowingly. "Pretty sexy stuff sometimes as well."

A little surprised that his friend was familiar with the subject, Pan was happy he hadn't told Hep just how sexy Nina's screenplay was likely to get. From the sounds of things there would be several sex scenes but at least she wouldn't be starring in them.

For a moment Pan wondered how she really felt about that. The evidence in the photo albums had shown her happy with her work. There was also what she'd said as they were packing her stuff, about how "variety was fun". Had she been talking about different kinds of sex with him, or had she meant something else, a variety of partners being something she enjoyed?

If so, she was doomed to disappointment. He wasn't about to share Nina with anyone. Sure he might have considered a ménage with her and someone else, like her sister Echo, in the past, but that was then. That was before he'd brought Nina into his life. She was his now, no matter who else she wanted, or who wanted her. Pan had no intention of playing well with others, not where his Nemesis was involved. She'd just have to content herself with him as a lover.

But what if it wasn't enough. That nagging thought haunted him. He wanted to keep her with him even after the spell wore off. Could he do that and keep her to himself at the same time? Would she be content to stay with him alone, or would he have to learn to share what he wanted to keep?

"Hey, Pan," Hep said. "You have something on your mind?"

He looked over to see that his buddy was watching him with a concerned look on his face. Pan suppressed a sigh. He couldn't even hide his feelings from Hep, not noted to be the most observant man in the world.

Normally he'd have no trouble hiding his thoughts from others. Nina must have gotten under his skin worse than he'd expected.

On the other hand, Pan reasoned, maybe he should level with the god, at least a little. After all, the man's advice so far had been pretty solid, getting her to move in with him and having the laptop made. He didn't need to tell Hep everything…like about the adult film Nina was making. Still, it was no secret Nina had been busy in the bedroom.

"Well, remember how you said that I'd find out a lot about Nina from her place?"

"Yeah, I did." The big man's eyes turned pensive. "You find out something you didn't want to know?"

"Sort of. I knew she'd been pretty active sexually. Had other partners."

"You find out she had someone special? A rival?"

"No, nothing like that. But she was a lot more active than I'd expected." He grimaced. "Maybe even more than I had been."

"Really? More than you? Wow, I wouldn't have thought it possible. She'd practically have to make a whole career out of sex to do that…" Hep's obvious admiration broke off as Pan glared at him.

The big god cleared his throat. "I can see how that would bother you, but it's all in the past, isn't it? It isn't like she does that now, right?"

True enough, but that wasn't really the issue. "It isn't that she does anything about it but I worry that she might miss the...variety."

Hep took a deep swig of beer then fixed him with a steady stare. "Do you miss the 'variety'?"

"No, but I'm not the one in question here."

"Did she say she missed it?"

"Not exactly. But I think she might. I was wondering..."

Hep threw up his hands, a look of horror on his face. "Hey, buddy, we're friends, but don't go thinking about including me or Apple in your love life. I'm strictly an observer here and we don't 'swing', as the humans put it."

"That's not what I was going to ask anyway," Pan said with disgust. "I like you, Hep, but I'm not going to share Nina with anyone. That's the problem, I don't want to include anyone else in our bed."

"Oh, okay." The big man sighed with relief. "I see where we're going. So you want to include some variety in Nina's life, but not make it another lover. Interesting problem." Hep sipped his beer and pondered for a while. After a moment he leaned forward and looked at Pan speculatively.

"How do you feel about toys?"

Pan shrugged. "Toys? You mean like whips, handcuffs, and dildos? They have their uses." In spite of his concerns a smile crossed his face as he thought about the large box Nina hadn't let him see the inside of. She had hidden it in the bottom of her closet as soon as she'd gotten it home. What was in that little surprise package? he wondered.

"I know Nina likes them."

Hep grinned. "I have something a little more elaborate than an inanimate object in mind. Suppose you could get some 'variety' without it being a real person. Would that be of interest?"

Someone that was more a toy than a real person? At least Nina wasn't likely to prefer such a thing to him. He leaned forward, intrigued. "Maybe. What kind of a toy?"

Grinning, Hep finished his beer and slammed the mug on the table, which shook under the big man's force. He gestured for Pan to finish his beer. "Drink up. We need to see a man about a statue."

* * * * *

Astonished, Pan stared at the carved marble figures in the sculptor's workshop. "Wow. They look so lifelike." One was a man at the height of his beauty and youth, the other a high-breasted maiden. They were beautiful even though they were made of cold stone.

He turned to their beaming creator. "Pygmalion, these are wondrous statues."

Pleased, the little man smiled at the god's compliment. "I'm glad you appreciate them. They are the inspiration of a lifetime."

A sculptor known for his ability to create realistic figures, the ancient Cyprian had outdone himself this time. These were even better than the man's most famous statue, Galatea. Not that Pan would ever say that out loud. It wouldn't be a wise thing given the circumstances.

Pygmalion had sculpted Galatea then fallen in love with her stone figure. He'd asked Aphrodite to give him a wife like the woman he'd sculpted and she'd answered his prayer by turning the figure to life. Pan might think these figures fairer than the man's wife, but the sculptor would never see them that way.

To a man, his wife is always the most beautiful. Or should be.

"How does Galatea like them?" Hep asked and Pan cringed at the big man's bluntness.

To his surprise, Pygmalion looked embarrassed. He leaned forward and his voice got softer. "To tell you the truth, it's become a problem. She didn't seem to mind when I was working on them, but since they are finished she's done nothing but complain about how big they are, how naked they are…she wants me to get rid of them. I think she's a little jealous of them," he said confidentially.

"Hmm," Hep said. "What you need is a good home for them. Maybe someone with a large garden where they wouldn't seem so out of place."

All of a sudden, Pan realized what Hep was suggesting. He took another good look at the statues. He knew how to turn figures like this to life. That was the solution Hep was suggesting, to use these figures as stand-ins for the lovers he would no longer allow Nina to have.

Of course, he'd only make them come to life when they were wanted for sex. Otherwise they'd become too human. He would have to be sure to treat them as sex objects only.

For a moment he considered the maiden's breasts and what it would be like to suck on those beautifully formed nipples. Oddly enough they didn't appeal nearly as much as Nina's did.

Still, he wasn't doing this for himself. It was Nina who wanted variety in her lovers and using these statues could be the answer to that need.

"I'd be happy to give them a place in my garden," he told Pygmalion. "You could visit them when you like."

The little sculptor rubbed his hands together, obviously pleased at the solution. "That's wonderful. Galatea will be so pleased." He stared at the pair of stone figures. "I can't imagine what I was thinking of when I made them."

* * * * *

In Titanous, Hyperion watched Pan and Hephaestus converse with the sculptor with rising amusement. He smiled as Pan waved his hands and magically transferred the statues to his home.

When this was all over, he'd find a way to repay Pygmalion for his unknowing assistance. The man had been ridiculously easy to influence into creating the figures. He'd managed to make one of them the exact double of his beloved daughter and her guard. Not that he was completely happy with who that guard was, but the man had volunteered. The key thing was that the statues were now in a place where someone was likely to turn them to life.

Raising his fists in an enthusiastic cheer, Hyperion stopped his hands just short of hitting the low ceiling. He glared at it for a moment then returned his attention to the worlds below.

His plan was under way and things were working out just fine.

Chapter Five

Nina glared at the kitchen wall. The blank space next to the stove was made of woven, living branches still green with leaves. It would be an excellent place to store her new pots and pans if she had a set of pegs to hang them on.

On her computer was an image she'd found on a home design website of a lovely kitchen, complete with a pot rack. It looked both functional and decorative, a great solution to storing her presents from Echo.

She wanted one just like it.

The garden wasn't cooperating. She'd tried six times already to get the wall to grow pegs for her pot rack, each meeting with dismal failure. Either the incantation wasn't right, or her focus wasn't right…something was wrong.

Of course she could ask Pan to build her a rack as soon as he was home, but she'd wanted to be the one to accomplish the task. After all, how hard could it be to convince a living wall to make pegs? Some of the branches were already nearly the right length and position. It should only take a little effort and would be a good test for how much she'd learned about working in Pan's garden.

Well, maybe the seventh time would do the trick. Nina straightened her shoulders and raised her hands into the position Pan had shown her earlier and directed her stare onto the thin green branches of the wall. In her mind she pictured a set of pegs at equal intervals, each long and thick enough to support one of the pans.

She closed her eyes and spoke the incantation. *"Garden glorious, green and good, do my bidding as you should."*

When she opened her eyes, the wall was shaking and for a moment Nina was thrilled that this time she might have actually done it. Her smile faded when she realized that instead of the short branches growing into pegs, they were actually shrinking back into the wall. It was as if the garden was deliberately thwarting her.

She leaned closer and listened to the leaves shaking, then frowned. It sounded like…giggling? The garden wall found this funny?

Outraged, Nina shook her finger at the quivering wall. "Are you laughing at me?"

As if in answer, the wall grew even smoother, the leaves settling into place with an expression she could only describe as smug. Nina was being dissed by a bunch of foliage. This would never do.

Narrowing her eyes, Nina leaned in to talk to the wall. She pitched her voice silky smooth, but with an edge of danger. "I know I'm new here, but I'm planning on spending a lot of time in this garden. Pan wants me to make this my home, too, and that means having you pay attention to me. If I can't learn Pan's methods, I might have to investigate others."

The leaves lifted away from the wall, as if listening to her. Nina suppressed a smile and added a sinister note to her voice. "You know that I've spent a lot of time on Earth. The humans have non-magical ways of coaxing nature into doing their bidding, particularly in their gardens. They use tools to shape their plants. Like stakes…ties…trimmers"

The wall shivered a little.

"Sometimes they even have power tools for really big jobs…like hedge clippers."

Now the wall visibly shook. Nina shrugged. "Now I'd hate to have to resort to something like that." She eyed the wall. "For example, to hang my pots I'd have to get some pieces of wood and a hammer to pound them in. I'd put them right here, and here…" She used her finger to indicate the places she wanted pegs.

A profound shudder went through the wall and then short branches sprouted along the exact line where Nina hoped to put her pot rack, every place she'd pointed to. They grew to thick three-inch long pegs in a matter of minutes, perfect for her purposes. Nina smiled and ran an approving hand along the leaves. They fluttered and preened under her caress.

"I'm so glad we understand each other now," she told it in her most soothing voice. "I'll be talking to you later about the new benches in the pool area."

She could almost swear she heard a resigned sigh come from the wall.

Nina was putting her pots away when she looked up to see a haze develop in the middle of the garden. She headed from the kitchen area to investigate only to find that there was now a pair of marble figures taking up the center of the plush lawn, nearly hiding the small duck pond behind them.

Lovely statues, but what were they doing in the middle of Pan's home? Honestly, she wished he'd ask her before redecorating the place. If she were going to be living here indefinitely, it would be nice to have some say, particularly when it came to life-sized statues. They were nice and all, but they did take up a lot of room.

Pan arrived a few minutes later. He didn't even glance at the statues, but instead set a small keg on the table and drew a nice tumbler of amber ale from it.

Still wondering about the new additions, Nina took the glass and sipped appreciatively. "I see you've visited the smith."

"I did. He sends his regards. Wanted to know how the laptop was working out."

"The machine is wonderful," she told him. "I finished the intro and the entire first story, 'The Genie and the Fisherwoman', this afternoon." She glanced over at the statues in the middle of the lawn. "That was before these arrived."

Pan grinned at her. "Do you like them?

"Well, yes…" Frankly she wasn't sure what to think about them. "They certainly are…large."

Pouring himself a tumbler, Pan pulled her out onto the lawn. "They are life-sized. Created by Pygmalion himself."

"Oh?" Nina examined them more closely. The statues really were exquisitely made, every curve lifelike. Even the expressions on their faces seemed alive. She could almost believe them actual people, frozen in space and time rather than carved stone. For an instant, she thought she saw one of the eyelids on the female flicker, and her chest move. Nina stepped back instantly. Could they be ensorcelled as her sister nymph Echo had been?

Pan was still grinning at her. "I was thinking you could use them in your work."

Nina turned to stare at him. "How?"

"Well," he said slowly. "Sometimes you want someone to act out a scene but if we do it we tend to get…distracted."

Nina grinned. She knew just what he meant about getting distracted. That had turned out to be one of the best parts of this entire exercise.

Pan returned her smile then nodded at the statues. "I thought we could use the statues and have them act your scenes out instead."

Suddenly Nina saw his plan. "You're going to bring them to life? To act out my screenplay?" She clapped her hands together. *What a great idea!* She could have them be the Sultan and Scheherazade, the Genie and the Fisherwoman, The Kalandar Prince and the Lonely Widow…

"That, and other things. I remember what you said about enjoying variety."

Enjoying variety? Nina's heart sank. Surely he didn't mean… "You want to have sex with them?"

"I thought we could use them that way. Kind of like sex toys. But not just me. You and me…and one of them…maybe both." Pan's voice sounded strained even though he spoke as if he were talking about the weather, rather than adding another lover to their bed.

It was hard to hide her disappointment. This was exactly what she'd been worried about with Pan. Already he was bored with her and looking for new bodies to bed.

She'd thought that he'd wanted her and her alone and now he'd not only gotten one extra person for sex, but two. And one was male! She'd thought Pan was no longer interested in having male lovers.

On the other hand, since what they'd done in the morning was most often associated with homosexual love…maybe he did miss having a stiff cock around in addition to his own. Nina eyed the male statue's member. It would likely be pretty impressive when erect.

It certainly couldn't be denied that the figures were beautiful and would probably make excellent lovers. Nina decided that she probably should be grateful that he'd brought people of stone into their home and not living souls. She didn't feel grateful, though.

"Something wrong, Nina?" Pan seemed to have caught her changed mood. Better not to act as if anything bothered her. If he wanted to play it cool and bring others into their relationship, better these sex objects than real people.

With care she hid how miserable the idea made her. Maybe if she just thought of them as animated toys…not that that would be much help. After all, she'd named her first dildo Hector. It had been long, thick, carved of wood and painted a deep purple. For years it had given her satisfaction until it had finally split in two during a particularly strenuous workout. She'd been in tears when she'd laid Hector to rest after a century of use.

Even inanimate objects could become cherished in time. Nina glanced at Pan and wondered if he'd ever really care for her as much as she had Hector. She could only hope so.

Certainly the female statue was such that most men would become fond of her. A beautiful face, long curling hair, and even in her current state of cold, hard marble, it didn't take much imagination to see her as a voluptuous woman. Nina could almost imagine how she'd look when turned to life. She'd be any man's wet dream, especially Pan's.

Obtaining them to please her…sure he had. Nina wasn't nearly naïve enough to believe that. Still, what was she to do? She couldn't very well openly complain about his gift. After all, it was her pictures from the *Dodi Does It* series that had given him the idea of bringing in extra bodies to fuck in the first place. He clearly thought she wanted more than him.

Nina snuck a peek at Pan, still openly admiring the statues. What would he do if she told him she didn't want anyone else? Wouldn't he see her as needy and pathetic?

Even if it was true, she didn't want him knowing it. A woman had to have something when a man left her. Pride, if nothing else.

Nina took a deep drink of her beer. It really was excellent, a testament to Pan's exceptionally good taste. The truth was he'd shown great taste in selecting statuary as well.

She'd just have to make the best of things. He'd suggested they use the statues as actors in her play and that wasn't such a bad idea. She could use them that way, have them work through her scenes and make love to each other. She had no objection to them doing that. She might even be able to find a way to restrict them to those love scenes and keep them out of anything involving her and Pan.

"I don't find them that attractive," she told him. "And I'd have to see how they act before I'd agree to anything else. They might be too stiff to work out."

Pan looked pleased. "I suppose you are right. Let's get started," he said, moving toward the statues. Curious as to how the god was going to actually make them live, Nina observed carefully.

Taking position behind the stone figures, Pan placed one hand on the back of each of their heads. He chanted slowly.

"Figures of stone, hard and cold

Come to life as was done in old.

Cast off rigid form and be

As pliant as true flesh can be."

A shudder seemed to run through each of the marble figures and as Nina watched color blossomed in the stone of their hair and skin. The color spread along the torso and limbs, the male considerably darker than the female, a rich chestnut brown to her light tan. Soft dark hair with tight curls appeared on the male's head, while the female's shoulder-length hair turned a fluffy pale red, the color of a dawning sky. Eyebrows and lips colored to match, as well as the hair covering their sexual parts. They blinked their eyes and the white irises filled with sky-blue on the woman and near inky black on the man. In unison, they turned their heads to each other, and their lips parted, revealing teeth still the marble white of before. Near identical smiles appeared on both faces, as if they knew some secret that Nina could only guess at.

They were just statues, she told herself, made by an artist whose skill was near god-like. That was why they seemed to have such strong personalities as they became living flesh. There couldn't be any other reason.

Stiffly at first, but then more fluidly, each figure stretched from the near crouch it had been in, straightening limbs with audible creaks and cracks.

Where the two statues had been now stood a man and woman, both of them nude, both watching Nina with rapidly narrowing eyes. Nina began to wonder if this had been such a great idea Pan had had. In her experience, statues-come-to-life didn't always behave as you expected them to.

Obviously not sharing her concerns, Pan strode around them to stand in front with her. "Aren't they wonderful?" he asked, pride evident in his voice. "Could you ask for a better pair of subjects?"

Well, they certainly were magnificent, Nina had to give him that. The woman stood about medium height, her apparent age about mid-twenties, with the voluptuousness of a full-grown woman, not the young girl she'd originally thought her to be, heavy breasts and still narrow waist. If Nina had been casting for the part of Scheherazade, this woman would have been perfect.

The male was just as perfect. His dark skin made a nice contrast to the red-haired woman's paleness, and Nina could picture in her mind how luscious the pair would look making love. With a practiced eye, she examined his cock and was happy to see it was uncut, perfect for the part of an Arabian prince. While significantly smaller than Pan's mighty organ, he was still reasonably well-endowed.

Yes, the pair would make great stand-ins for the actors she'd need to play the parts in her screenplay, assuming they could take direction. She still worried about the likelihood they wouldn't.

In addition there was the matter of the male's glower at Pan's comment. Whoever or whatever the statue was, he had a mind of his own and didn't take well to being told what to do. She almost warned Pan to watch what he said to the pair. But then a bland expression took over the female's face and she kneeled before Nina and Pan, gesturing to her fellow statue with a gesture so subtle that Nina almost didn't notice it.

Her suspicions rose a little. What was going on with these two?

Reluctantly, the dark-skinned male joined her on his knees in the soft grass.

"Oh master and mistress, how may we serve thee?" the red-haired former statue said. "We were made to do as you request."

Her male companion shot an angry look at her, but said nothing.

Pan beamed, turning to Nina. "You see, they're exactly what we need."

Need where? In their bedroom? Inwardly she cringed until she heard his next words.

"All that's needed is your script and we can have them acting it out in no time. They are the perfect pair of actors for you."

Nina drew a sigh of relief. At least at this point Pan wanted to use them for her screenplay instead of his own sexual gratification. Who knew how long that would last, but she could hope it lasted quite a while. In the meantime one way to avoid Pan thinking about sex with them was to get them dressed.

"Maybe you could magic them some clothes, Pan, something appropriate for an Arabian sultan and his wife. We wouldn't want them to catch cold," she said, gazing meaningfully at their exposed bodies.

* * * * *

Pan watched his woman with a growing dread. Was Nina thinking about sex with their new playthings already? He'd just turned them to living flesh and she was already giving them the benefit of her professional stare. Nina ran an evaluating gaze up and down the now living bodies. Did her stare fix a little too long on the male's genitals?

He suppressed a groan. Perhaps bringing the statues into his home hadn't been such a good idea. Obviously she liked them…maybe even more than he'd hoped. She wanted to put clothes on them. That sounded like she wanted to treat them like real people, which was not what he'd wanted. If they were real, she might fall in love with one of them.

The next thing you know she'd want to name them…

"What are your names?" Nina asked.

Pan withheld another groan as the male and female looked at each other in obvious puzzlement. They were just statues, not real people. What would they be doing with names?

"Names, mistress?" the female asked.

Crossing her arms, Nina gave the pair an impassive stare. "Yes, names. I want to know what to call you."

Male and female exchanged glances. With a shrug, he spoke first. "My name is Ast…"

"Aster," the female finished, giving the male a sharp look. "His name is Aster and mine is Dawn."

Pan grumbled to himself. It was time to get involved and remind them who was boss. He couldn't let the statues forget he was the one to give them life. He needed to control them and make sure nothing happened that he didn't approve of.

"Dawn," Pan repeated. "A lovely name for a lovely lady." He took her hand and kissed it, trying not to pay attention to the intense look the dark-skinned male was giving him.

He was grateful to see the even more intense look Nina gave him. Good, let her feel a little jealous, that would only make her appreciate him more. He didn't want to seem too caught up in her otherwise he'd risk her becoming bored.

If Nina knew just how much she meant to him she'd be gone from his garden before he could stop her. Yes, this was the best course, to keep things casual.

Even it if killed him.

Dawn took her hand back from him, a look of near annoyance on her face as she returned to her feet. Aster was quick to be by her side, his attitude somewhere between protective and threatening. As the bigger man loomed over him, Pan wondered if this really had been the best idea he'd ever had. Or the best idea Hep had ever had, since it really had been the smith's suggestion that Pan give these no-longer-stone figures a home.

As he thought about it, he realized it was probably a good sign that Nina wanted to put clothes on them. Naked, they really were too much of a temptation, both for him and for her. Pan sketched his hand along their bodies and immediately fibers from the air appeared to knit themselves together into clothing. Long harem pants and a tight little bodice for the statue named Dawn, tunic, vest, and pants for Aster, her male counterpart. For both the fabrics were rich, velvets, silks, and satins, appropriate for a sultan and his queen.

Looks of astonishment followed by those of appreciation were evidenced on the former statues' faces. Dawn's smile seemed genuine as she rubbed her hand along the fine velvet of her bodice.

"I'm dressed like a queen!"

Aster stood proudly, folding his hands across his now-covered chest. "And I'm a king." He certainly looked the part with his chin held high in the air. He turned his steady stare on Pan and he felt a measure of menace surrounding the no-longer-stone man.

If ever there was a man destined to play a homicidal sultan, Aster had been made for the role. Hopefully all murder would remain part of the fantasy and not become reality.

Dawn finished admiring her new clothes and faced them. "You mentioned a play?" she said with a bright smile. "Something you need help with? What can we do to help?"

Chapter Six

Aster frowned at the sheaf of papers in his hand, his handsome brow knotted in concern. "I see that I'm supposed to want my new wife dead every morning, but I don't understand why I'd do such a thing. What's my motivation?"

"Motivation?" Dawn glared up from her copy of the script, a look of disgust on her pretty face. "Your 'motivation' is that you're a selfish pig. Can't keep a woman satisfied with just you, so you have to kill her. Typical male behavior."

Eyes narrowing, the man returned her glare. "No woman has ever been dissatisfied with me."

Nina stifled a groan. Had she expected a pair of statues to have smaller egos than human actors? If so, she'd certainly been wrong. If anything Dawn and Aster had at least the number of issues and questions as the normal actors she'd worked with, and in some ways far more.

For one thing, she'd never had an actor question her on whether or not he needed to be naked during a sex scene before. Usually she had to coax her male porn stars into leaving something to the audience's imagination, but once clothed Aster had become reluctant to take anything off. She had no such problems with Dawn, who was happy to be dressed or undressed as the occasion decreed.

She had other problems, however, because for some reason the newly made woman had taken a seemingly instant antipathy to her co-star and reveled in annoying him at every opportunity. This, of course, made directing them in a sex scene a special kind of experience, akin to shoveling snow in Hades' underworld. No sooner did you lift a heaping spade-full from the ground than it melted into water that ran off the blade, freezing when it hit the earth again.

As soon as she explained one part of the scene to her fledgling thespians, obtaining their grudging approval on it, they found disagreement with another. It was enough to make a budding screenplay writer insane. Of course she had to be crazy to fall for Pan's scheme anyway. Not that the god was around to see the fruits of his brilliant idea. He'd taken off as soon as she'd handed out the scripts and started rehearsal, claiming a previous engagement.

An engagement involving Hep and more of his amber ale, she was certain of it. Pan had left her to deal with the situation, a situation that was his idea and his making. Imagine taking two stone statues and turning them into actors! She was lucky their performances weren't stiffer than they were.

As it was, there was a certain woodenness about them… No, she should stop that line of thought before it petrified on her. The last thing she needed was to make her concerns concrete. It was bad enough they were set in stone…

Nina shook her head and attempted to rid it of the rest of the bad puns that had infested her consciousness. *She was a playwright, not a bricklayer…*

This had to stop. None of this was getting the first scene of her play worked out. Clearing her throat to get their attention, Nina pointed an impatient finger at the pair and put on what she hoped was her stoniest expression. "Quiet down, both of you, or I'll have Pan turn you back into statues immediately," she said.

She was gratified to see that the threat actually worked. Eyes wide, both Aster and Dawn gave her their complete attention.

Putting on her most imposing attitude, Nina waved her hands nonchalantly. "It's a very simple scene," she said, hoping she projected more assurance than she felt. "Dawn, you are Scheherazade, the sultan's new wife. He's lying on the bed and you come into the room. You bow to him as a proper wife would..." Nina opted not to make comment on how Aster grinned and Dawn rolled her eyes. "...then you remove your clothes. Do it slowly, one fastening at a time, one garment at a time. The idea is to tease and tempt."

Aster took his position on the cushions they'd put on the lawn to represent the sultan's bedroom and lolled against the back pillows, his attitude in keeping with his royal status. Nina had to admit that he looked pretty good that way. Now if she could just get Dawn to cooperate.

Raising his arms, the "sultan" clapped his hands twice and spoke his first line imperiously. "I wish my bride to attend me." He frowned ferociously and only the tilt of one of his eyebrows gave away how amused he was by the entire state of affairs.

On cue, Dawn entered the area Nina had marked out as the stage, ducking her head appropriately when she faced him. Even her bow looked good, Nina thought, if you ignored the slight look of disgust on her face when she did it.

"I am here, my lord and master. How can I please you?"

Aster's eyes twinkled and Nina realized he was enjoying his role. "I desire entertainment, woman." His gaze ran along her body. "Disrobe for me, I would see the beauty I bring to my bed this night."

Fire flashed in Dawn's eyes, but she did as she'd been directed to do, carefully removing her garments one piece at a time. First she unlaced her tight bodice, letting her nipples show through the opening before pulling it off her shoulders and slipping it to the ground. With a smooth movement she slid from her shoes and worked her waistband down her hips, naked breasts swaying with her efforts.

It wasn't the seductive striptease of a professional dancer, but Nina decided that would have been inappropriate for a virginal bride on her wedding night, as Scheherazade would most certainly have been. Instead Dawn played the role as a shy woman taking her clothing off for a man she didn't know, a man who would soon be her lover and, if her plan to entice him with her stories was unsuccessful, a man who would order her death in the morning.

It was a complicated relationship to be sure and as Dawn took her clothing off, Nina grew more impressed with the woman's insight into her character's role. There was clearly more going on in Dawn than she would have expected from a mere statue.

Aster watched her performance with an appreciative gleam in his eyes, and as Nina watched the front of his loose pants got considerably bigger. She made a note on her copy of the script to add into it Dawn's interpretation of Scheherazade's disrobing. The innocent striptease was just what the scene needed.

Clad only in the briefest of undergarments, a thin and transparent wrapping of her most private parts, Dawn walked to her "husband", her hips swaying in acute invitation. Aster gave a near growl as she came closer, then groaned as she put a hand on his chest.

Dawn broke character and turned to Nina. "Should he be doing that?" she asked. "Moaning and groaning like a schoolboy with his first woman?"

The mood shattered and Nina couldn't resist a groan of her own this time.

Blinking in annoyance, Aster sat up straight. "Now just a minute, that's hardly fair. After all, it's been a while..."

Never mind having the sultan kill his wife, Nina was going to do it for him! Here they'd just gotten into the scene and Dawn had to interrupt, spoiling the mood. Nina took a deep calming breath, resisting the urge to scream.

"You're right that he shouldn't be reacting quite that strongly, but I think we can let Aster have a few groans at this time, even if they aren't in the script. This is a run-through, not a polished performance. I just want to see how the scene goes and not everything needs to be perfect."

She pointed to Aster. "Lie back down and don't worry about keeping quiet. If you want to groan, do it. Last thing we need is performance anxiety. You—" Nina redirected her attention to "Scheherazade", the perfectionist. "You pay attention to what you need to do and leave the directing to me. It's my job, after all. I want you to touch his chest, and ask to see it. He'll say you can and then you'll take his shirt off. Understand?"

Both nodded, and they began the scene at that point, Nina taking notes and directing them. Aster's breathing picked up, but he bit down on his lips, canceling any groans, moans, or other audible sounds of pleasure at her touch. When she licked his dusky nipple, he made a small hiss but quickly suppressed it. Mischief blossomed on Dawn's face and after that it was clear she was working to get a reaction out of him in addition to his steadily increasing erection.

Stifling the urge to interfere with Dawn's game, Nina watched as the other woman pulled on "the sultan's" pants, freeing his erection. The script suggested that Scheherazade go down on him, but Dawn merely teased Aster's cock, drawing the foreskin back and licking it carefully. Aster gave up any attempt at stoicism and moaned under her ministrations, his hands wandering to her back then moving to find her breasts. He in turn teased her nipples with his fingers and it was Dawn's turn to make noises deep in her throat. She whimpered when he released her breasts.

Aster smiled at this minor victory and pulled her down onto the bed next to him. Trapping her on the soft surface below him, he took the lead in their lovemaking, apparently oblivious of Nina's rapt attention. Aster's pants fell off the bed followed by Dawn's undergarment, ripped from her un-protesting body. Now he lay gloriously naked on top of an equally nude Dawn, the pair of them kissing with a passion at least equal to the energy they'd expended so far in irritating each other.

For all of the pair's arguing and teasing, it was clear they were compatible sexually. Not for the first time, Nina wished she had a video camera to film them. The way they heated up when making love, they'd be perfect as her main characters in her film. Unfortunately she would have real trouble getting them into Actor's Equity given the fact that they were living statues rather than flesh and blood humans. A pity, really. They were better performers than most of the porn stars she'd worked with, at least in these roles, and she loved how his dusky coloring contrasted with her pearl-like skin. Nina began making a mental list of the darker skinned actors she knew who could take Aster's place.

In the meantime, Aster seemed to love Dawn's skin, running his hands over her breasts like he held the most precious of jewels. He raised one of her legs to fall over his shoulder, opening Dawn's sex to his and Nina's rapt gaze. One of his hands delved between her folds, making Dawn moan with heightened desire.

Nina muffled her own moan of sympathy, keeping as quiet as she could to avoid disturbing the pair. They seemed oblivious to her now, too engaged with each other to be worried about having an audience. As a result their performances were perfect.

Now Aster pulled Dawn's legs apart on the bed, settling himself between them, supporting himself on his knees. He gazed down at her with an imperious look, the look of a sultan about to claim his bride. He took his cock in his hand and smoothed it, using his own fluids to make it slick and ready for her. Dawn's eyes grew wider as she watched him, and Nina could see the start of a protest cover her lips.

It was a protest she never was able to deliver. Aster held her thighs firm as he moved abruptly forward, spearing her with his massive shaft. Dawn cried out at his entry, and Nina could almost believe she had been a virgin when they'd begun.

He didn't stop, but bore into her, covering her mouth with his own, his groans covering the rest of her cries. Finally joined, they paused, Aster's limbs shaking with the effort to keep still, Dawn's entire body trembling on the bed beneath him.

He pushed himself up and stared down into her face. "And now, my bride, you belong to me, and me alone."

Whatever response Dawn might have had was lost in what came next. Aster moved in her, his cock grinding into her, at first slow, then steadily faster as he found what tempo worked best for them. Along his back, his dark skin grew damp as they coupled and Nina could see a faint sheen of perspiration dotting Dawn's face as well.

Aster shuddered and stopped, pausing in mid-stroke over her, his entire body shuddering with the effort. Clenching his jaw, his eyes closed for a moment, as if relishing the feel of his upcoming release. From beneath him came Dawn's hands trailing down his back in a sensuous caress that ended on his round buttocks. Her fingers smoothed across them, then clutched at the firm mounds with frantic need.

"Please, my lord. Don't make me wait any longer." Her voice seemed no louder than a whisper, but it carried clearly to Nina's ears in the stillness of the garden.

No longer able to hold out, Aster resumed pumping into her and with a loud cry, emptied himself deep inside Dawn. While muffled by his chest, Dawn too cried her pleasure and finally both of them lay still, their breath coming hot and heavy.

Nina put one hand over her mouth, trying to control her own breathing. It had been a long time since she'd witnessed a sex scene that profound, and it had made her more than a little aroused.

Not that she wanted to join Aster and Dawn on their makeshift bed, but if a certain hairy-legged god were to show up soon, she'd be all the happier for it.

As Nina continued to watch, Aster raised himself over Dawn's body and stared down at her. "Why have you done this to yourself? You are lovely, Scheherazade, with a body as fine as any I've known before. But I've seen beautiful women before and held their bodies close to mine. No matter how desirable I find you, tomorrow I will order your death. You knew this, and yet still you came to me. You were not forced. Nay, I heard you asked to come to me, to become my bride even through you knew you would die as a result. Why would you do this?"

Dawn looked up at him, her gaze as intent as his. "It is simple, my lord. I seek to change your mind about killing me."

"And how would you do that? Yes, you are lovely, but other women are as lovely as you. Many are more so. Many are better at the art of love than you. So what do you offer me that I can't find elsewhere?"

"It is true that other women are more beautiful than I am. They are more voluptuous, more tempting to a man of your refined tastes. It is also true that I'm not the most proficient at the erotic arts, although I'm sure I can satisfy your desires. But what I can offer is unique to me and me alone, my lord. In my mind are stories, enough to fill a thousand and one empty and quiet nights. That is something you will get from no other woman, my lord.

My tales are exceptional, exciting, and beyond anything you've heard before."

She smiled shyly at him, letting her hands caress his face, tracing his lips. "I am unique among your brides, my lord, because I will satisfy both your hunger for the flesh—and the mind."

The "sultan" frowned, but did not immediately deny her words. "It has been a long time since a woman challenged me to find more than her body of interest. You say your tales are the equal of those of the greatest bards? Very well, Scheherazade, I will take your challenge. Entertain me with one of your stories. Perhaps I will let you live so I might hear another."

"Oh, my lord, my stories are not short tales to entertain for the moment only. They are epic legends of wonder and intrigue and are not the kind that can be told in one night. If I begin a tale it will take the rest of the hours until dawn and still not be completed."

His gaze grew more intense, his interest now obvious to the watching Nina. Aster sat up and pushed pillows behind his back, making himself comfortable. "Very well, my many-worded bride. I'm in the mood for a legendary tale of wonder. Begin it now and if I find I cannot bear to live without hearing its end, I will spare your life in the morning."

Drawing about her a thin robe, Scheherazade also sat up on the bed. She arranged herself into a comfortable position, took a fortifying sip of wine from the goblet near the bed and when she was ready began her tale.

"My story, great lord, begins on the beach near a small fishing village. There was once a young fisherwoman who was very poor, but very, very wise..."

Dawn's voice trailed off and both she and Aster broke character and looked over at Nina. "That's the end of the scene you gave us," she said.

From the shadows behind Nina came applause and Pan stepped into the light. "Wonderful job," he told them, "simply wonderful. Well done by both the actors and the writer." Aster and Dawn looked pleased and Nina smiled, cheered at his approval.

"How long have you been standing there?" she asked.

"Quite a while. I came in while they were making love and didn't want to interrupt." He wiggled his expressive eyebrows. "Very good scene. But then that last part was the best."

She'd just written that section into the script that afternoon. "You thought it was good?"

Pan smiled broadly. "It was excellent. I particularly liked the part about how she tells him that while he's had many women, it is her mind that makes her unique. It sets everything up so that he can't help but evaluate her as more than just a body to warm his bed."

From the air he conjured a tablet and paper and Nina could see it was full of writing. "I just had a couple of notes for the actors."

While he went through his list with the attentive pair, Nina watched him and pondered what he'd said.

More than just a body to warm his bed. That's what Nina wanted to be for Pan. Did he see in the sultan a bit of himself, a man who went through many women, rarely staying with one for any length of time? As far as she knew, she was the longest to occupy Pan's bed, ever. Of course it was because of the arrow, but she'd noticed how Pan sometimes seemed to enjoy her company as much out of the bedroom as he did inside. He was even taking an interest in her activities and helping with her script—and was doing it with enthusiasm!

On the other hand she was still aroused from watching Dawn and Aster make love. At the moment pursuits outside the bedroom were far from her mind. She slid up to Pan and put an arm around his waist. He broke off what he was saying to give her his attention, his narrow eyebrows raising quizzically.

"Do you want something, Nina?" he asked.

She smiled at him. "As it happens, yes." Her voice was pitched to make it clear just what she had in mind.

Pan's face grew guarded. "What about our friends here? Shall we ask them to join us?" The reluctance in his expression didn't encourage her to agree.

She was happy to say no. Nina spared a glance at the former statues, the pair watching her with intent expressions. "Not now. They've had enough exercise today. I think it's time to return our actors to their normal state for now."

A look of relief crossed his face then he gestured to Aster and Dawn to rise. They obeyed although Dawn did so reluctantly and Aster wore a mutinous expression as he took his position on the lawn.

Standing behind them, Pan waved his hand. *"Flesh to stone as you were before, until we need you living once more."*

Pink and brown skin paled to the same color of marble, and the pair were frozen in place again. Belatedly Nina realized that Dawn was still wearing the thin robe Pan had made for Scheherazade's costume, but she decided it didn't look so bad. In fact, having Dawn's beauty covered seemed a lot better than having it available for Pan to lust over.

"Maybe I should have given him a robe too," Pan muttered.

Nina turned to him. "What?"

The god drew her slowly into his arms. "Nothing. Just thinking aloud." He nuzzled her neck and ran a line of delicious kisses down her throat, his beard tickling the sensitive skin. "Now, what did you want from me?"

* * * * *

In Titanous, Hyperion entered his throne room, only to find Helios sitting on the all-seeing throne, a pensive smile on his face. The smile disappeared when Hyperion caught his attention. "Father. What mischief have you been up to?" He waved his hand at the image of Olympus far below them. "And what plans do you have that require my sister to put herself in danger?"

"A statue in a garden? She's hardly in danger."

"She's wasn't a statue a moment ago." The pensive smile was back on Helios' face and he even chuckled a little. "I will admit she wasn't exactly suffering from the experience."

"Aphrodite turned them human already? Let me see!" Hyperion gestured to his son to exit his throne and the younger Titan stood, reluctantly giving up the seat. The Titan king frowned as he saw the two figures turned to stone.

"Pan changed them, not Aphrodite." Helios crossed his arms and frowned. "You are planning to do something to the goddess of love?"

Hyperion returned his son's glare with a look laced with malicious mischief. "I'm planning on getting us free, one way or another."

"I've told you that Hephaestus has offered to help us win our freedom—"

With an imperious wave, Hyperion interrupted him. "I know what you said, boy. I'm not about to negotiate with the Olympians. It's always been war between us and it always will be."

"After five thousand years, I'm scarcely a boy, Father!" Helios scowled. "And things have changed. The Olympians don't spend all their time making war any more than the humans do. Clinging to old ways won't help us." He shook his golden head in frustration. "If you would only listen—"

"So long as I'm king of the Titans we'll do things my way, and that's the old way!"

For a long moment, the two Titans exchanged glares, then the younger one clenched his jaw and bowed his head into a shallow nod. "Very well, Father. We'll do it your way...until someone forces you to see reason." He turned and exited the room, leaving Hyperion to glower after him.

Chapter Seven

Back on Olympus, Nina reached for and cupped Pan's bulging loincloth. "Oh, I don't know," she said, massaging his balls gently. "What comes to mind?"

A short whoosh of air left Pan's throat. "Well," he said through gritted teeth. "We could go over my notes."

With her hand caressing his engorged cock, Nina had lost track of their conversation. "Notes? What notes?"

"The ones I had for the statues. I wasn't all that impressed with the way that scene went. With the lovemaking."

They'd done a fine job as far as Nina was concerned, but who was she to argue with an expert. Besides exploring his "notes" had real potential. "So, why don't we go through the scene ourselves and you can show me what they should have done?"

Pan seemed happy to oblige her. "To start with I think perhaps the sultan's bride might need a little persuasion to be placed in his bed. After all, she knows it's her death he's got planned."

Nina grinned at him. Now this had *real* potential. "Persuasion?"

He loomed over her, letting his size speak for him. Nina felt the intensity of his attention, his overwhelming masculinity, as the force it was. If nothing else, Pan was pure male sensuality on the hoof. Literally in his case, she thought, staring down at his cloven feet.

Pan grabbed her hands and held them effortlessly with one hand. Scooping up one of Dawn's dropped silken veils, he wrapped it around Nina's wrists, securing them together. She barely had a chance to bleat before he picked her up and deposited her on the cushions that had recently been the "sultan" bed. With one quick motion he secured her bound wrists to the edge of the bed above her head, then used another pair of veils to tie her feet loosely to the bottom edge.

Nina didn't remember there being hooks in those locations on the makeshift bed, but with Pan's magic in his garden he could easily add what he wanted, where he wanted it. There were some advantages to making love to a god.

He stood over her, eyeing her still clothed body with thinly veiled delight. "And now, little nymph, I'll show you how a real man of power makes love to a woman."

She couldn't help an anticipatory giggle. Secured to the bed Nina wriggled her hips in delight. "Oh, please, my lord. Be gentle with me."

Pan ran his hands along her side, speaking a set of short sentences, obviously some kind of spell. The seams of her top separated and the garment fell off her in pieces. With one hand he collected each piece and pulled it from her, letting some of the silken fabric drag across her skin. Now nude from the waist up, Nina's nipples peaked under the combination of cool garden air and his hot, sensuous assault.

Pan stared at her breasts, his breaths coming short. "So beautiful. I can never get over how lovely your breasts are, Nina." His hands cupped their fullness, his fingers stroking the soft skin.

Arching her back, she pushed them deeper into his hands. "Is this the way a sultan torments his captive bride, by playing her breasts? Surely you can come up with something more inventive than that."

A grin took over his face even as he shook his head in mock dismay. "You are still the mouthiest little wench I ever met. I think I'll give you something to occupy that tongue of yours." His loincloth flew to one side, and he lifted Nina's head and pushed his cock into her mouth. Accepting it eagerly, she sucked on it and ran her tongue along the head. Straddling her chest, Pan rubbed his ass along her breasts, catching her nipples with every stroke.

Nina moaned around his cock, already rock-hard and filling her mouth to the brim. She'd never been able to take all of him in, no matter how much she'd tried, and from this angle it was even harder to attempt. Either not caring or not understanding her inadequacies, Pan held her head and urged her to take more of him, the gentleness in his hands belying the harshness in his voice as he threatened dire consequences should she fail to please him.

"Take me, wench, or I'll…" Pan's voice trailed off in a gasp as she delved her tongue deep under his glans and swirled it around the head of his cock. "Oh, yeah…" he said appreciatively. "Do that again."

So she did and then did some other things with her tongue she hadn't gotten around to doing before. Thirty years in the adult entertainment trade taught a girl a few tricks, and for the first time Nina used every one she'd learned. By the time she'd run out of new ways to tease his cock with her tongue, Pan's eyes were glazed.

Pulling out of her mouth, he gave her the most intense glare she'd ever received. "Woman, I will get you for holding out on me like that."

She grinned up at him impudently and wiggled her bound fingers. "Imagine if I had my hands free."

"Oh, no. I've got you where I want you and that's that." With an impatient gesture, he waved his hands and the seams of her slacks suffered the same fate as her blouse. He pulled the now disconnected pieces away from her, revealing pink satin underwear with an enticing panel of sheer lace covering her woman's mound.

At least it should have been enticing, but Pan merely growled. "Underwear…why do you inconvenience me this way? That's another thing you'll have to pay for," he told her meaningfully.

The thought of what kinds of "punishment" Pan was promising made Nina's knees weaken and her pussy flood with anticipatory dampness. The garden air cooled the wet satin covering her crotch and it was almost a relief when he tore them off her. She couldn't resist a small sigh of regret when her underwear once again fell in pieces to the ground. She'd liked those panties.

It was a darn shame that Pan had this problem with underwear. At this rate, she'd have to buy up a lingerie store to keep outfitted unless she could get Pan to use his magic to make her some new ones. Not likely, since he proclaimed women's underwear to be a nefarious plot invented merely to get in his way. It was clear she needed to educate him on the joys of fancy underclothing.

Of course that would take longer than a few months. Briefly Nina wondered how much longer they would have together and if she'd get the opportunity to teach Pan about how fancy packaging could entice a man's attention.

Not that she was having any trouble getting his attention. Now that they both were naked, Pan stretched out and covered Nina's bound body with his own, rubbing his heavy cock against her soft curls. She felt his strength and desire and the control he had over her. He could do whatever he wanted and she could do nothing to stop him. It was thrilling but not frightening. Both of them knew that she was in no danger from him. Pan wouldn't really hurt her.

On the other hand, he would have some fun with her and that's what he was doing now. Stretched out on top of her, he rubbed his cock against the cleft between her legs, stimulating her clit into awareness. It was already throbbing, but Pan's strokes brought it to full alert and she moaned in response.

She tried to draw her knees up, to open wider and give him further access, but the soft silk veils tied around her ankles kept them fixed to the bed. Pan's face appeared near devilish as she writhed beneath him, desperate for relief from his too-teasing touch.

"Is there something you want, my captive? Something I could do for you?"

She wriggled her fingers and strained against her bonds. She needed someone to stroke her nipples and caress her breasts. She needed someone's hand between her legs, taking care of the ache in her clit. Bound as she was, it couldn't be her hand.

Nina was truly at his mercy. "Please, Pan. Touch me."

Pan planted a soft kiss on her forehead. "I'll do better than that, my little captive." He moved slowly down her body, inch by inch, using his tongue and lips on each part of her. He took his time. The length of her neck alone took him several minutes to traverse. Pan kissed and licked until she was ready to scream with frustration. He spent some quality time on her nipples, laving each with his special suckling before moving further down her body. On reaching the tender expanse of her belly, he took care in using the soft beard on his chin to tickle her belly button.

Finally he arrived at her most sensitive places, her clit and her pussy. Pan raised his head to stare at her face. Nina moaned when all he did for a few moments was blow puffs of air against the aching, swollen bud of her clit. The soft pressure from his warm breath provoked her. She wanted more than hot air from him.

"Please, Pan. I don't know how much more I can take." She sounded desperate and felt every bit of it.

"Oh, you'll take all of it, little one, eventually," he responded with a wicked grin, rising up to show her how big his swollen cock had gotten. Even after all this time, Nina's mouth gaped at the sheer size of him.

"For now I'll give you something a lot smaller but just as satisfying to think about."

He wiggled his long sensuous tongue at her, and then closed his mouth around her swollen nub, letting that talented organ go to work on her. If Nina could have broken her bonds, she'd have lifted off the bed at the intense pleasure of the sensation. Instead, helpless, she lay quivering under him, panting as he licked and laved her, giving her all of the benefit of three thousand years of practice. If Nina had thought herself an expert on oral sex, Pan was at least her equal.

In some ways, she had to admit, he was a whole lot better. For one thing, he never seemed to need to come up for air. Probably one of those other benefits of being a god, being able to control whether or not you had to breathe.

Certainly he was divinely good at this.

Nina whimpered as she felt an Olympian-sized orgasm begin like the first shivers of the land during an earthquake, then screamed her throat raw when it arrived. She shook and quaked like California during a 7.2, her mind collapsing like a building of un-reinforced bricks.

She was still trembling and barely conscious when Pan sat up and fitted his cock to the opening of her pussy. He waited, though, to drive home and only after she'd recovered a little did she realize that he too seemed to shiver with anticipation.

He smiled down at her, his brown eyes possessive. "And now, my lady, you belong to me." With one stroke he entered, filling her to her womb with his cock. Nina groaned at the sweetness of his heated entrance.

"So, good," Pan said, his voice a harsh whisper. "You feel so hot and wet. You are mine. Nina, tell me you're mine."

"Yes," she moaned. "Yours. Anything you want is yours." She'd give him anything if he'd just stay inside her for a little longer.

Pan stared down at her. "Mine." He said the word slowly then moved, a single stroke in and out that pulled on her pussy muscles, clenching tight around his cock.

She wanted that too. "Yes, Pan. Like that."

"Like that?" He grinned at her. Repeating the action, he took up a pattern of strokes, some long, some short, some fast, some slow. It was hard to predict what he'd do next and she loved the anticipation of meeting his cock with what limited movement she had. She couldn't direct him, was being held immobile beneath him. It was infuriating, exhilarating, and absolutely wonderful being under his mastery.

Nina wasn't used to giving up control to a lover. She'd rarely been the one tied up in the bondage scenes she'd played before. With Pan it was different. It was liberating letting him take charge. She loved how he took control of their lovemaking, of her body, and of her. Nothing could be better sensually than this, nothing she could think of.

Not that she was able to form much in the way of coherent thought at the moment. All she could do was react to the pounding of his cock into her, her body twisting underneath him. Around his cock her pussy contracted and she felt the swell of another massive climax coming. It came closer, closer…

"PAN!" Nina screamed, then moaned as he froze above her, his face triumphant. She shuddered, moaned again, and gave in to the miniature death, the only kind of oblivion an immortal was likely to feel.

Her pussy clutched tighter and Pan's triumphant expression slipped, replaced by a look she knew well, his look of impending orgasm. When he came his cry was nearly as loud as hers, echoing through the garden. Finally he collapsed on top of her.

It was several moments before either of them could lift their heads. When Nina opened her eyes, it was to see Pan watching her through half-closed lids, his expression fiercely possessive.

Not certain she was actually reading him correctly Nina stared at him in return. "Pan, is something wrong?"

He shook his head and the look in his eyes faded. "No, not really." His usual grin returned. "Just getting carried away." With a single jerk, he freed her arms from the bed then untied her ankles, and allowed her to sit up.

"It's always been a fantasy of mine to get you under my complete power," he continued, carefully not meeting her gaze.

Rubbing her wrists, Nina considered his words carefully. "I'm not used to someone having control over me. It can be…stimulating."

"Stimulating. An interesting way to put it." He drew her into his arms. "Perhaps we should explore this some more. "

"No more tying me up tonight." Nina showed the red marks on her skin. "Perhaps we can play another game instead."

"What did you have in mind?"

Nina pulled out of his arms and danced away from him. She struck a coquettish pose a few feet away. "Chase me to the bedroom, and I'll show you."

She didn't make it more than halfway there before Pan ran her down and threw her over his shoulder. Carrying her, he slowed down and strode purposefully to the bower.

"I prefer to save my energy for sex if you don't mind, little nymph."

"Oh, I don't mind," she told him as he ducked to enter the doorway to their bedroom. "Really I don't."

* * * * *

Once they were gone, the garden returned to its normal quiet, the only sounds the nighttime noises of the animals and birds living in the nearby bushes. In a few moments the soft chirps and squeaks were joined by more soft groans and moans coming from the bower.

In the silence around the stone figures, inaudible to all but the most sensitive of immortal ears, two voices began talking, one male and the other female.

The female spoke first. "So, what did you think of that?"

"That?" the male answered, his tone scornful. "On a scale of one to ten, I'd give it a seven point five."

"A score of seven point five out of ten?" She sounded amused. "Doesn't that seem a little low to you? After all, there was bondage and oral sex. Even we didn't get that far."

"Hmph. I gave them the point five for tying her up, but otherwise it would have been straight sex, hardly that inspiring. And he had the nerve to give me 'notes' on my performance," he grumbled.

"As for what happened between us..." His voice turned silky smooth with male satisfaction. "We were far better, even with the limitations of these bodies. What was between us was special and far more than casual sex, princess."

"Hush. Don't call me that!" She had a worried note to her voice.

"Why not? No one here can hear us."

"Still, we need to be careful. And I don't know what you mean about the sex between us being special."

"Sure you do. Didn't the universe move for you, my lady, as it did for me?"

"It might have shaken a little," she admitted slowly. "You are...bigger than I'm used to. And you have some nice moves."

"Nice moves?" he exploded. "That was world-class sex, woman! Just because I didn't go down on you…"

"Oh, very well. Yes, it was very nice. You are a very good lover, Aster."

"Don't call me that," he growled. "I'm not a flower."

"It's close enough to your real name and we need to be careful," she warned. "We don't want to give ourselves away too soon."

"How long must we stay like this?"

"Until the right time. What's the matter, do you find my company difficult?"

The male sighed. "You know how I've wanted to be with you, although being made of stone isn't much fun. It's hard to stay still when others are free to move about and enjoy themselves. I'm glad they moved out of sight. I don't think I could stand watching those two rut any longer."

"Patience. We must discover the secret of turning to flesh for ourselves. We lack both the knowledge and the power it takes. Unless we can control the process it will be difficult for us to act. Until then, we must behave like the innocent statues we appear to be. Just learn the nymph's lines and act out her scenes."

He laughed. "Her scenes are fun," he admitted. "And the acting is interesting. As assignments go, this is better than I could have anticipated." His voice grew tentative. "Besides, I do enjoy your company, princess."

"I'm…finding I rather like yours as well." She sounded surprised. "It would be best if we continue the charade of fighting, though. It will keep them off balance."

"If only we weren't made of stone…"

"...we won't be forever." Her voice sounded wistful. "And someday we'll be free. Free to pursue our interests anywhere we want."

"Freedom is worth any price," he agreed solemnly.

Chapter Eight

The screenplay was going great, even better than Nina could have predicted. After a month of working with Pan and her captive thespians, she'd finished all but the last scene, where the sultan realizes what a treasure he has in Scheherazade and grants her permanent immunity from his death sentence.

She couldn't be happier with what she had so far. The potential she'd seen in the story was playing out perfectly with the help of her two actors. The statues had done a fabulous job acting out her suggestions, to the point where Nina was seriously thinking of trying to use them in the final version of her film. It would mean transporting them to Earth and she'd have to get them human birth certificates and social security cards, but those weren't that hard to come by and it would be worth it. She might even get them into the Screen Actors Guild since they showed talents that went far beyond the bed as far as acting was concerned.

The pair of them were the best actress and actor she'd had the pleasure to work with in decades. Plus they really seemed to work well with each other, even if they spent their time not in character arguing with each other about one thing or another.

Nina had spent too much time in Hollywood to take these kinds of fights seriously. It was her experience that the bigger the fight between two people, the more likely the pair was screwing each other's brains out in private.

In this case, the screwing was happening in Pan's garden and only private in the sense that she was usually the only one watching. Whatever problems Aster and Dawn had, they disappeared as soon as the pair was given a script and a horizontal surface to work with. Then they demonstrated a real professionalism when it came to the art of love.

Or, Nina considered, it was possible that through their lovemaking they showed how they really felt about each other. It was rather hard to tell which, but she was beginning to lean on the side of the pair falling in love.

With a snort, Nina shook her head. When did she become such a romantic? Sure Aster and Dawn seemed compatible, but that didn't mean they were soul mates. After all, they were merely statues that came alive occasionally. It wasn't like the pair had souls.

Or did they?

Pan had assured her the statues were nothing more than stone made ambulatory flesh, but she wasn't so sure. Several times she'd caught Aster watching her with a cunning look that seemed to belie his supposed mineral origin. He didn't act like he had gravel in his guts.

Dawn wasn't exactly what she was supposed to be either. The woman had a royal presence beyond her beauty and youth, and her intelligence was anything but that of a woman with rocks in her head. Her companion had noticed it too. Aster watched her with awe as well as desire, particularly when he didn't think Nina was watching.

A princess and a warrior. If she didn't know better, that's what she'd have expected them to be.

But then again, Nina realized, she wasn't exactly what she was supposed to be either. She was Nemesis, the embodiment of opposition, vengeance, and retribution…or at least that's what she'd been before Pan had come into her life.

She gave a glance around her now familiar surroundings. Look at what she'd become…living in a garden with a god of the forests and fields, and barely thinking beyond her next opportunity to bed him. Like Pan she coaxed nature to do her bidding, not demanding it obey her. She couldn't remember the last act of revenge she'd been involved in.

Even her sex life had changed. Centuries ago she'd entered the world of adult entertainment as a way of getting control over men. Now her own sexual needs controlled her. All Pan had to do was wiggle his finger—or wiggle his cock—in her direction and she came running to do whatever he wanted.

Nina muttered gloomily to herself. She ran to him, forgetting who she was supposed to be. If she hadn't been so disgustingly happy she'd be disgusted with herself. As it was… She was a little disturbed by it.

With a sigh, Nina returned to her computer. She was working on the last scene of the screenplay, or what she was hoping would be the last scene. It was unclear because she wasn't sure just how to end the story. In the book she was using as a reference, many years had passed and Scheherazade had borne the sultan three sons. She had begged for her life for their sakes and the sultan agreed to pardon her. Afterward there had been a big wedding where she'd been installed as sultana and her sister married to the sultan's brother.

It was an okay ending for the book, suitable for the times in which it had been written, but Nina decided she needed something more modern. For one thing, she couldn't see Dawn begging anyone for anything, and the statue and her attitudes had become ingrained in Nina's perception of Scheherazade. In general she liked the idea of the wedding as an ending, but it was rare to put a wedding into a porn movie.

Instead she'd have to end with a sex scene and make it a real love scene for the characters. It was really the only good way to finalize the story. Something new would have to be introduced...perhaps Scheherazade was pregnant?

Nina blinked. Where had that thought come from? Scheherazade, pregnant—that wasn't bad at all! With sudden enthusiasm, she attacked the keyboard of the laptop, needing to type her idea into the computer before it slipped away from her.

Engrossed, she missed it when Pan returned, well after the Olympian sky had darkened and the stars were high.

He looked over Nina's shoulder at screen of her laptop and read aloud the first few lines that talked about the book ending of *A Thousand and One Arabian Nights*. "A wedding?" Mischief blossomed inside him. "That would be interesting."

Nina looked up at him in disgust. "I'm not ending an adult film with a wedding, Pan. Besides they are already married and it would be confusing to the audience to have a second ceremony."

Pan hid his disappointment. He didn't think it hurt to have official acknowledgement of a relationship but she was the film expert. "Perhaps you're right. So how will you end it?"

"I thought with her announcing her pregnancy, although that too is odd for an adult movie. Then they make love again."

"How are you going to make that different?" He thought for a minute then grinned. "I suppose you could add a ménage."

Nina favored him with a penetrating look. "That would hardly convey the message of true love, Pan, if they need a third person involved. In another scene that might work, but not this one." She shook her head. "I think it would be better if they made love again, only this time it would really be making love. He'd call her his perfect woman, or something like that."

Pan nodded, pleased beyond what he'd expected. So Nina didn't think having more than one body in a bed was needed. Secretly he agreed with her…he felt no need for anyone besides his little nymph.

"I like that, Nina." He leaned in closer and smelled her special scent. It had changed since being with him. In the past there had been a kind of spice to her smell, not completely pleasant, a trace of something almost like vinegar.

That was gone now, lost in the smell of flowers and growing things, a reflection of her position in the world he lived in.

Nina belonged in his garden now. He could look around and see the evidence of her presence, the soft moss-topped seating near the large bathing pool and modern human-styled kitchen in the corner. They were all changes she'd wrought in what had been his home…changes that made it her home as well.

He couldn't be more pleased at the result. Every day he felt like he grew closer to his goal of keeping Nina with him forever regardless of whether the spell they'd both experienced faded and failed. He didn't want to lose her, not now, not ever.

Perhaps he might ease into the subject of their continued relationship. Pan leaned over her to touch the keyboard. "It's getting late. Perhaps you could finish this tomorrow. Hep and I were working out in his shop and I could use a bath. If you come with me, I could use someone to scrub my back…amongst other things."

Nina smiled at the obvious invitation in his voice, but then nodded her head at the statues, who'd gone to stone overlooking the pool. "What should we do about them?"

His heart seemed to freeze in his chest. Was now the time she wanted to invite these others to join in their lovemaking? It had been over four weeks since he'd brought them here and in all that time she'd not said a word about having a ménage. He'd hoped she'd forgotten about it.

But it had been his suggestion and he wouldn't back out now, not if that's what it took to keep her happy. Pan tried not to let his disappointment show in his voice. "Did you want them to join us this time?"

Nina closed up the laptop and turned to him. "I meant that they could see and hear us in the bathing area. And no," she said firmly. "I don't want them to join us. I never want them to join us, not the way you mean."

Her jaw set and Nina stared into his eyes. "Pan, I'm tired of you asking that. I never wanted them to have sex with us in the first place."

"You didn't?" Surprise filled him. "But I thought you said…about variety…"

"Not in lovers, Pan. I've been there and done that and am not interested in going there again. You're the only lover I want."

Pan's heart felt like it would leap from his chest. "Then what shall we do with them?"

Nina looked over at the statues. "For now they are good at acting the screenplay out. When that's done—well, we'll see. All I know is that eventually I want them out of the garden. Having them here…it's almost like having an audience to everything we do."

She took a deep breath. "I don't want an audience, or other lovers, Pan. When I talked about variety…I meant other things. Things we haven't done."

This was intriguing. Was it possible he'd missed something? "What kinds of sex haven't we done?"

"Well…" A deep blush crossed her face, something Pan had never seen before, and it fired his passion. What could Nina be thinking of that would cause her embarrassment?

"When you brought a man into things," she told him her voice hesitant. "There was something I thought you might like."

This had to be good…no, this had to be great if it was making Nina uncomfortable. Pan hid his anticipatory grin and simply nodded, keeping his expression as stoic as possible.

"So…what do you want me to do?"

She actually squirmed. "Well, maybe it would be better if you started that bath without me. I'll join you in a minute."

Pan stared after her as she strode purposefully toward the bower. Heading for the bathing area, he pulled off his loincloth, leaving it on one of the benches. He waved a hand at a pair of widely spaced tall tapers and they lit up with a soft glow, illuminating the bathing area with a romantic light that reflected off the dark water. Pan smiled at the effect. Perfect.

He stepped into the water, onto the low steps in the heated end of the pool. With a thought he turned up the temperature in the pool so it was steaming by the time he was chest deep. Mist rose off the surface and into the air, obscuring the surroundings so he could barely make out the candle flames. If he couldn't see out, then others couldn't see in and that should put to rest his suddenly shy nymph's concern about being watched.

Pan chuckled to himself. *Imagine that.* Here Nina was used to performing sex in front of millions of people through her cable television program but now she was uncomfortable having a stone statue observe them as they made love.

Making love. Pan sighed and looked through the haze to the barely visible stars above. That's what he wanted to do with Nina tonight. She might not remember it but it was six months to the day that he'd jumped in front of an arrow, attempting to save her life. It had been the most impulsive act of his life and it turned out to the best move he'd ever made. He didn't want to wait to see what was real between them anymore. This love he had for her had to be real, as real as it got.

Tonight he'd make it more than real. He'd make it permanent. After tonight there would be no more guessing as to how long Nina would stay, or when she would leave. If he had his way, the answer would be forever and never, in that order.

Pan was on the cusp of a great decision. He intended to take a certain sexy, exasperating, and mouthy nymph to be his wife. The bulk of Olympian society might be shocked at his choice to give up his never-the-same-woman ways, but he knew what was important to him. He wanted Nina, now and always, and he'd do anything to keep her...including the commitment of marriage. He wanted her committed to him with the same bonds he felt for her.

Nina's voice came from the shadows beyond the candlelight. "Pan? Are you in there?"

He floated back into the relaxing hot water. "Here, Nina. Are you coming in?"

"In a moment." She wandered closer and he could see she was wearing a robe. Again there was that strange hesitancy in her voice. "I'd rather you not see me until I get in the water."

Oh really? Pan's eyebrows nearly met the bottom of his horns. What was his little nymph up to? He tried to keep the eagerness out of his voice. "Should I turn my back?"

"If you don't mind."

Whatever it was, it had to be something very unusual. She had something sexual on her mind, and it wasn't something Nina had done with just anyone. If it had been she wouldn't be acting so strange.

This was something very different, even for her. Pan grinned. He couldn't wait to find out what.

"Very well. I'll look the other way."

"Promise you won't peek?"

A hard thing to promise given how curious he was, but what the Hades. He'd do anything to keep his Nemesis happy. Resolutely Pan turned in the direction of the garden wall, away from Nina's approach. "I promise, Nina."

He could hear her steps on the grass, then the fall of her robe onto the bench where he'd left his loincloth. A short gasp escaped her as she entered the water, then there was a long sigh as the warmth soaked into her skin. "That feels so good."

He couldn't help his satisfaction in her pleasure. "It's meant to feel good, Nina. All things between us should feel good."

Her laugh sounded short and, to his ears, insincere. "We do feel good together, Pan. But feelings can be just that. Not real but an interpretation of reality."

She couldn't be more wrong in this case. "I know what I feel, Nina. I want you, and I know you want me. There is nothing left to interpretation between us."

Nina moved closer to him, her body hidden by the dark water of the pool. Her hair had grown to her shoulders since coming to live with him and she'd pulled it up off her neck into an unruly pile. Candlelight glinted in the depths of her dark eyes. Pan read uncertainty there, but something else as well. Was it possible Nina really cared about him?

That's what he thought he read in her eyes. Love…

Surprise widened her eyes and he realized he must have said the word aloud. He repeated it, putting more emphasis on it.

Nina shook her head. "Not really love. It's just lust, Pan. Arrow-enhanced, but nothing more."

There was more to how he felt about Nina than lust. He knew lust, had known it for thousands of years with any number of women. Lust came and went, was hard to control, but it left your heart alone.

Nina brought out in him something he'd never expected to feel, honest emotions that sometimes scared him at their intensity. Just the thought of her leaving gave him an anxious feeling in the pit of his stomach, something he'd never expected to feel about a woman. There were times he felt as if he would rather die than lose her.

It was more than lust, but he wasn't going to argue with her now, at least not with words. He'd let his actions carry the message to her, to tell her how he really felt about his little nymph, and when that message had been delivered, he had another one for her, one just as important, possibly more.

She was still a few feet away in the pool. Pan moved closer to her, stalking her quietly as she watched. For a moment he thought she was going to back away, but she held firm, her face glowing in the candlelight that filtered through the mist rising from the warm water.

Reaching her, he took hold of her shoulders and pulled her close enough to place his lips over hers, a kiss he hoped held less passion and more of the his depth of feeling for her. He put it all into that kiss, as much feeling as he could manage. Under the water his cock was hard enough to pound nails, but he kept his lips soft on hers. She'd see there was more than lust on his mind.

She let him pull her into his arms, pressing her body against him. The familiar feel of her fired his blood. He ran his hands down her, caressing her soft breasts and toying with her already pebbled nipples. She was excited and ready for him already.

Pan reached for the juncture of her legs to stroke her clit. Perhaps they'd make love in the water. It wouldn't be the first time, but repeating old favorites was always fun.

He sought the hard sensitivity of her clit, but found something else instead. Something unexpected, and something that most certainly shouldn't be between Nina's legs.

Pan broke off his kiss and stared into Nina's now wary face. He cleared his throat carefully, not sure how to ask the question in his mind. Finally he decided directness was the best approach.

"Nina...do you by any chance have a penis attached to you?"

Something that might have been laughter sped through her eyes. "Well, actually...yes, I do."

His hands wandered down the hard erect member to where it joined her body and found first one leather strap, then another. She wore a harness of some sort, probably the new cock's support system. Pan breathed an inward sigh of relief. At least it wasn't a permanent addition to her body.

The corners of her mouth twitched upwards. "It's a strap-on dildo, Pan. Something from the box of tricks I brought from my apartment."

Pan pulled her hand down to his erect member and guided it along his length. He liked the way her eyes lit up with desire as she felt just how big and hard he was. "Why did you think we needed an extra one, Nina? Isn't mine enough for you?"

She licked her lips and it was all he could do to not pounce on them.

"This cock isn't for me, Pan. It's for you."

"For me?" Now he was surprised. "And what do you think I want with an extra..." his voice trailing off as he caught the gist of her idea. Then he remembered her concern over Aster and his jaw dropped open.

"You thought I wanted Aster to fuck me?" He couldn't decide if he was outraged or if he wanted to laugh. Perhaps both.

"Well..." Nina's voice trailed off as she caught the trace of his anger. "It's not like you haven't had a male lover in the past. I thought you might have missed it."

"Missed getting buggered, you mean? And so you were going to fuck me instead. With this." He gave the dildo a tug and was gratified to see her pulled towards him. Well, if nothing else, it made a good handle.

She looked completely chagrined now. "I guess it was a bad idea. I didn't mean to upset you."

A bad idea...that was one way to put it, Pan muttered to himself. He'd never been so insulted. He gave the false cock another caress. Imagine him having something like that inside him. Hard and long, and thick...it would fill his ass completely, probe deep inside him, caress his prostrate like a friendly finger.

Nina would have to enter him from behind and he'd be submissive to her. She could lie against him, her breasts soft against his back. Her hands would be free to caress him, and maybe play with his cock as she stroked deep inside him…

Pan broke off his sensual imaginings as a sharp thrill went through him. A long-ago memory rose of a man who'd been his lover for a while, a very short while. Their relationship had been iffy, he remembered, but the sex had been great while it lasted. His asshole clenched at the memory of his friend's hard cock taking him deep and slow.

Deep and slow. Pan closed his eyes and a further rush of excitement flooded his body. It had been rare that he'd allowed a man back there and he'd never had a woman want something like this, but he had to admit…now that he was thinking about it, getting fucked in the ass didn't really sound all that bad. The more he thought about the better it sounded. In fact, it was sounding pretty interesting.

And after all, Nina had gone to all the trouble to dig out her rig and get dressed up for him, fastening all those straps and everything. And she'd wanted to please him and thought of this as a way to keep him from wanting another lover.

That was interesting in itself. Nina wanted to be any kind of lover she thought he wanted? Why shouldn't he take advantage of something like that?

Pan used the cock to pull her into his arms and tilted her chin up so her eyes met his. She looked as if she wished she were anywhere else.

"I suppose you remembered to bring the lube out," he said gently.

It was worth it if only to see her jaw drop open. Pan withheld his laughter as Nina struggled to understand his change of attitude.

"You mean you want to…to have me…" She gasped for a moment. "You mean that you want to try it?"

He broke into a grin. It wasn't often that Nina found herself lacking words but he'd managed to overcome her powers of speech this time. Not bad for a god saddled with a mouthy little wench for a lover.

A mouthy little wench he was very much in love with.

He leaned in to kiss her, deep and meaningfully. Nina responded with all her usual enthusiasm, plus some. Her face was flushed, her heart beating fast as she pressed herself against him. This promised to be a first for them in more ways than one.

Pan didn't think he'd ever seen Nina so turned on. He wasn't far behind her either.

"You didn't answer my question. Did you bring the lube?"

It was hard to tell in the candlelight but he thought she was blushing. "Of course. It's over on the bench with my robe."

He gave her a little shove towards the steps. "Why don't you get it then?"

Pan watched as she climbed out and grabbed the familiar tube. It was water-based so they'd need to be out of the pool. With a wave of his hand, Pan transported a set of cushions next to the water, then climbed out to join Nina, now standing with an uncertain look on her face.

The cock she wore jutted proudly out from her crotch, an odd sight given how feminine she was otherwise.

Without thinking about it, Pan grabbed it and used it to pull her towards him. He grinned down at her.

"This is coming in pretty handy. I kind of like leading you around."

She matched his grin and gave him a push towards the makeshift bed. "Over there, lover. Lie on your stomach."

Giving up control to her wasn't easy, but it was part of the game. Even so, a little uneasy, Pan settled onto the cushions, his ass towards her.

Nina approached from behind. She was breathing so hard he could hear every breath, and he could smell her arousal even more. His cock grew harder, a surprise as he hadn't expected that was possible.

There was a soft noise, the sound of the lube coming out of the tube, then Nina leaned in to spread his ass cheeks wide, her fingers playing with the tight puckered opening. She was surprisingly gentle, even more than he'd noticed before and it relaxed him somewhat. This apparently wasn't her first time at this. That wasn't too surprising given her previous occupation. Probably if he'd looked carefully at her photo albums he'd have found her in a similar rig. Pan tried not to give in to his jealousy at the thought of some other man getting fucked in the ass by his little nymph.

She began whispering sweet, sexy little endearments while she probed his anus with her fingers, gently slipping them past the tight ring, coaxing it open. When her probing finger found his prostrate, the pressure became so sharp he almost climaxed. Immediately she eased off, letting him recover.

But only for a moment, and then she was back, this time letting him feel the tip of the artificial penis in place of her fingers, sliding it back and forth along his ass crack. She stopped at his opening, pushing forward just a little, a hair, the smallest amount. The head eased his ass open a little.

At this rate they'd be working all night. Pan swallowed hard, then pushed back and impaled himself onto Nina's lubricated cock. Her surprised gasp was almost louder than his grunt.

It felt…amazing. Just a little pain, only at first, then the satisfying feel of being packed full of a heavy cock, surprisingly realistic for a fake. He continued to push against her until he could feel the front of her thighs on his ass and knew he'd taken all of it into him. Then he settled forward onto the cushions, bringing her with him.

Nina lay over him, her breasts pressed against his back, her nipples pebbling against his skin. It was a strangely erotic mixture with her breasts on his back and the hard cock inside him.

Definitely not something to be missed.

"Are you all right?" she whispered to him as he panted against the cushion.

"Oh yeah." He was better than all right. "I'd forgotten…how this felt."

Without seeing her face he could feel her triumphant grin. "I thought you might like it."

Like wasn't the right word, but no matter now. Time to get on with it. "I'd like it even more if you'd move," he told her.

She started slow and easy, and he could feel her strokes deepen with every thrust. He couldn't resist pushing against her, particularly as his cock was being buried in the cushions beneath him, the softness pressing against it, making it ache. She rubbed her chin against his back, kissing the skin, nibbling gently, then not so gently. Her teeth left small tracks of sensation on his back.

He needed more…something…more of something. His cock throbbed from the blood pooling in his groin. Through gritted teeth he cried Nina's name.

"Touch me, woman."

She wrapped her arms around his waist, and her hand unerringly found his hard member. Nina stroked it, still murmuring encouragement into his ears.

Like he needed encouragement. Pan clenched and came hard in her hand, his cock pulsing under her fingers. Nina milked him dry, her fingers sliding over him while she kept up her steady strokes into his ass.

Reaching behind him, Pan grabbed her hips and stilled her movements. "Enough…that's enough." She waited for a moment, then slowly pulled the dildo out, easing her exit with the same care she'd used putting it in. Pan appreciated her efforts although they were hardly necessary. He wasn't particularly fragile or an innocent in any of these games. Not that he'd tell her that, at least at the moment. It was too much fun having her be careful of him.

Having her care to be careful of him. He hoped it meant she really loved him, even if she'd never said the words out loud. Actions often spoke louder than words anyway.

As soon as she was out, Pan reared back and grabbed her, then flipped her onto the bed beneath him. In startled bemusement she stared up at him as he suspended his weight over her. Well, most of his weight, anyway. He used his pelvis and thighs to trap her beneath him.

In spite of how hard he'd come, his cock was aroused again immediately. Funny how that was—he seemed to have a permanent hard-on when it came to Nina. No one else had ever kept his attention this long, and she certainly had his attention at the moment.

More to the point, he had hers as well. A look of near fear crossed her face as he stared down at her.

"So, my cock-toting lovely. You ready for me?"

She didn't have the chance to nod, he'd already lifted her legs high and speared deep. The strapped-on cock bobbed against his abdomen, a strange sight, but he ignored it in favor of staring at her beautiful breasts.

Nina moaned aloud as he penetrated her, then louder as he put up a furious pace, in keeping with the intensity of what he felt at the moment. Later he'd probably ache but not now. He wanted his little nymph moaning underneath him, as loud as he'd been with her inside him.

He wanted to blow her mind the way his was blown and he had just the cock to do the job. Pan pounded away into Nina, wringing moans, groans, and sobs from her. She cried out once, but he didn't stop or even slow down as her orgasm made her shatter beneath him. She came again, then again, but it wasn't until the fourth time that his own peak reached.

Pan came like a force out of nature, his cries near deafening as he shouted her name into the air above her head. Then he collapsed on top of her, letting his weight crush her for just a few moments. Better for her to know just what she was getting in him. Pan was not a man to trifle with. He wasn't a man like those she'd toyed with in the past, any of those who'd been in her photo album. He wasn't someone she could leave on a whim.

Pan was a god, a god who was bound and determined to have her with him.

He'd use anything he had to do it, his cock, his magic, even his weight to keep her. Gravity was his friend at this point. Nina wasn't going to be able to move until he let her move.

She stirred beneath him and it occurred to him that she might be having trouble breathing, so he lifted enough to give her air. His own breath caught at the expression on her face, a mixture of love and joy. Her cheeks were still pink with their exertions, but her smile was pure sweetness. Whoever would have thought that Nemesis could look sweet?

It was the face of his woman, freshly pleasured…and apparently exhausted. The lids of her eyes dipped and closed briefly as she relaxed under him. Enthralled at her beauty he watched her face clear and relax, then stared in astonishment as moments later a soft snore erupted from his beloved's lips. Nina had fallen asleep.

Pan couldn't help his rueful grin. Of all the situations for a man planning on a serious chat with his lover about their future. He'd worn the poor woman out with their lovemaking and their conversation would have to wait until tomorrow.

Something hard was poking him in the stomach. Pan sat up and realized it was Nina's strapped-on dildo. He raised a hand to get rid of it by dissolving the straps then hesitated. She probably was fond of this toy of hers. Laboriously, but with care to avoid waking her, Pan found the small metal buckles and for once used conventional means to remove the harness from her. He laid it on the cushions before settling next to her and cuddling her close in his arms.

What a woman. Capable, fun-loving, and a joy to be with, to live with, love with, and fuck. It had taken thousands of years to realize what she was to him, but then again maybe if he had known earlier she was the one, he'd have found a way to screw things up. As it was it had taken an arrow to drive home what she meant to him.

He'd stepped in front of her to save her from Aphrodite's wrath, certain that the goddess had intended on killing the nymph. In the moment he saw the bow raised, he'd envisioned an Olympus without Nemesis in it, and he hadn't liked the look of that world.

Pan freed her black hair from the clasp on top of her head and let it fall against the pillow. He stroked the glossy silk with a tender hand.

So much loveliness that would have been lost to Olympus if she'd died. A beauty that he'd claimed and now kept for himself. And he intended to keep her for himself now and always.

Around them the candlelight flickered, a sign that it was growing late. Pan waved his hands and the light went out, leaving them in a misty darkness. Standing, he gathered his sleeping nymph into his arms. The night would be too cold to sleep out here. Reluctantly, Pan headed for the bower and the comfort of their warm bed.

A sigh erupted from him over his aborted plans. Between the mist and soft candlelight the atmosphere near the pool had been perfect, an excellent stage for discussing the future. A pity that things couldn't have been settled tonight, but tomorrow morning would work just as well.

*****

In the growing silence of the garden, the dispersing mist from the pool drifted over to the statues, briefly encompassing them and giving their solid forms the illusion of movement. Aster seemed to blink and Dawn's lips appeared to part in the release of a soft sigh.

Inaudible to the hearing both divine and human, the spirits trapped within the stone whispered to each other.

"Well, what did you think about that?" Dawn said.

A grumbling growl of approval came from Aster. "I'd have to admit…that was a nine. Maybe a nine point five. I've never seen anyone make love that way before."

A snort of annoyance came from his companion. "I wasn't talking about their having sex, Aster." If she could have rolled her eyes, they would be spinning in their sockets. "I can see how you might have found that the most significant thing, you being a man and all, and it was impressive, I must admit. But I was talking about they said before they made love. Nemesis doesn't want us here after she's finished her screenplay. From the looks of things with Pan, he'll be happy to move us someplace else."

"Oh, yeah. I remember hearing her say that." Aster's voice grew grim. "Since she's on the last scene, it sounds like we don't have a lot of time left."

"No, we don't." Dawn sounded worried. "If we don't make our move soon, we could be left as statues for a very long time. I…I wouldn't like that. To be left like this, so close to you…" her voice trailed off.

"…So close to you," he finished for her. "But unable to touch, to taste, or to caress." She could feel his frustration grow even if he was made of stone, and half expected the smooth marble to crack from the tension inside him. "I would love to put my arms around you right now, to kiss you."

"Aster," she began slowly. "Even if we were in our normal forms, we could not. There is no future for us."

"No. I don't believe that. When this is over, we will have the opportunity to make things work between us."

"My father…"

"…will not come between us! Not after this past month. I have loved you and intend to keep on loving you, now and in the future. I would risk anything to have you with me, princess. You know that."

"Aster…" She let her voice trail off. She couldn't say anything more. He knew the problems but refused to let them thwart him. He'd always been like that, fearless in the pursuit of what he wanted. And now he wanted her and would take on her father to get her. To her chagrin, she wanted him as well. It would pain her to lose him, possibly as much as it would upset him.

One of the reasons they'd waited this long to act against the Olympians had been an unspoken desire to remain together in any form they could. Once this interlude was over she would never see him again, at least not the way she wanted to. Better to be stone part of the time than eternally apart. But if they were moved into storage on Olympus or, gods forbid, separated from each other, they wouldn't even have that.

Their only hope was to win freedom for their people, and earn her father's gratitude. Maybe if they succeeded they could have the relationship they wanted.

"Aster, we must look for the next opportunity we have and be ready to act. The time must be now—we can't delay any longer. It will have to be tomorrow if at all possible."

"I agree." Dawn could hear determination in the grim tone of his mental voice. "I'll be ready."

They would both need to be ready to act, but that was tomorrow. Dawn allowed herself to relax. Sleep wouldn't come to them in this form but there were other ways to spend their last night together.

No reason not to spend the rest of the night in other activities. The kind of enjoyable activities they'd discovered over the past month.

"Aster," Dawn said quietly. "Talk dirty to me."

His grimness faded away, replaced by loving amusement.

"My pleasure, princess."

Chapter Nine

Pan was holding her when she woke, his arms around her waist, legs curled around her body. It was rather like the way she'd held him last night when she'd entered him and the memory brought a flush to her face. It had been a long time since she'd worn or used a strap-on, and she'd never used one with a man before.

Certainly she'd never done it with someone she cared about. It had taken most of her courage to suggest it to Pan in the first place and she'd been certain he was going to turn her down angrily.

Instead, even though at first he'd been taken aback, he'd agreed to try it. The results had been...surprising. Pan had come so hard she'd expected him to be out of commission for a week. Instead he'd been inspired to give her the fucking of her life, so much so that she'd collapsed afterward and had actually fallen asleep!

That hadn't happened to her...well, in centuries. In fact she could only remember one other time it had happened. That had been the first time she'd gone to bed with Pan, three centuries before, when they'd first met.

That had been the most amazing week of her existence. In one marathon session of lovemaking he'd blown away every preconception she'd had about sex. Up to then Nina had been reticent about the act, unwilling to give up any kind of control to a man. She'd kept her pleasure to herself, barely even noting the fact there was another person in bed with her.

Some men had called her frigid…although never more than once. Nina grimaced at the memory. After all, she'd been a vengeance nymph. Bad things had happened to any man who'd insulted her.

But then Pan had come along. At first she'd tried to keep her passion in check, but it had been a fruitless effort. In the first ten minutes in his bed she'd had her first orgasm with a man. The second came five minutes later.

An hour later she was screaming his name. By the end of the first two days she'd known that she'd found her heart's mate, the one man in history that she could love, then and forever. Pan hadn't declared his love for her, but she knew he would eventually and so she'd unshielded her heart and given him all the devotion she'd held inside.

Five days later he'd left her bed and taken up with a vestal virgin he met after an extended stint at one of Bacchus' wine tasting parties. From what Nina had heard later, the little bitch had decided to change her life and picked Pan as the changer.

He'd shown up the morning afterward, disheveled and full of apologies over what had happened. His excuse of being drunk hadn't gone over well with her and they hadn't spoken more than a few words since. Until six months ago and the arrow, that is.

Nina sighed. Did Pan ever think about those long ago days? Probably not. When she'd brought up his past infidelity, he'd dismissed it as irrelevant to their current situation. *It would never happen again*, he'd told her. He wasn't the kind of god that dwelled on the past, but seemed determined to live in the present, maintaining only a moderate interest in the future. Somehow she doubted that would ever change.

He stirred behind her and his hands clutched tighter around her waist, pulling her against his already hard shaft. So what else is new, Nina thought. Pan always awoke with a hard-on.

"Good morning, sweetheart," he whispered in her ear. "You must have slept well. I didn't get a chance to thank you last night."

To her horror she blushed even more as he turned her towards him. His slightly devilish brown eyes glinted with humor, mixed with the ever-present desire she saw in them.

He touched her flaming cheeks. "Who would ever think the ever sexy Nemesis could be embarrassed about anything. There is no need for that. What happens between two people in the name of passion cannot be wrong. I enjoyed last night, more than I could have expected. You did too."

Grabbing her hands, he pulled them over her head, leaning in to nibble her lower lip. "On the other hand, there is something very appropriate about your blushing."

"What do you mean?" Pan was acting very strange. He rarely spoke in riddles.

His smile hadn't even the hint of mockery in it "There is something I meant to speak with you about. I was going to bring it up last night in the pool, but we got distracted."

Pan sounded serious, belying his smile, and it put an uneasy feeling into her. What did they have to talk about that would make Pan smile and be serious at the same time?

Some of her concern must have communicated itself to him because he pulled back from her. "Don't you want to make love?" she asked, looking for some semblance of normality in their relationship.

"Maybe later. I have a proposal for you first."

A proposal? "What are you talking about, Pan?"

He looked away from her. Perhaps he didn't want her to see his face. "It has been six months since you've been with me. I find…I like having you here. We match each other, get along well, and enjoy all aspects of being a pair, especially sexually. If nothing else, last night proved that." He hesitated in what sounded like a well-rehearsed speech. "I'd like to make it permanent, Nina. I want you to be my wife."

"You want to get married? To me?" She couldn't have been more astounded if he'd announced he'd decided to take up celibacy.

"Why not? We live together, are seen as a couple by the others. A formal declaration seems warranted."

"But, Pan, the arrow's spell. You only want me because of that. When it fails, you won't want to be saddled with a wife you don't care for anymore."

With a wave of his hand Pan seemed to try and brush her concerns away. "I'm not so sure the spell is going to fail, Nina. We've been expecting it to for months now, and it's as strong as ever. It may not ever fail, and even if it does, what does that mean? If the spell fails I'll still care for you, I'm sure of it. I don't think I'm so bespelled that I can't see how right we are for each other."

She shook her head vehemently. "I don't think we're that right for each other, Pan. I could never betray my word. I may be many things but I've never been dishonest with anyone. You on the other hand…I know you too well.

Once the spell fails, you'll be off chasing other women and I couldn't live with that. If I was your wife I'd have to."

Pan narrowed his eyes at her. "I wouldn't betray my vows that way, Nina. I care for you too much."

"That's the spell talking, Pan. You feel that way now because of it, but if you were free of it you'd betray me just like any other man would. You forget how long I've lived in the world, and I've seen very few men keep their word past the point of first infatuation."

"I'm not just any man. I'm a god, Nina. My word is good."

Nina's laughed insolently. "Don't tell me that, Pan. You forget how long I've been around. Gods aren't that different from other people. They fight and scheme and cheat. Your word isn't any different from any other male's."

Pan's face showed cold fury as he stood and strode away from the bed. He grabbed a loincloth and threw it around himself. "I'm sorry you have such a low opinion of men, Nina. I'm even more disappointed that you could count me among those who would hurt someone they love."

He headed for the exit from the bower.

"You don't love me, Pan," Nina called after him. He didn't stop, just continued on his way, and it infuriated her. "And besides, why shouldn't I count you that way? You're the one who gave me my first lesson in betrayal, three hundred years ago."

Now he stopped and she saw him flinch at her last words. For long moments Pan stared at her. "You really can't get over that one mistake I made. No matter how long ago it was, what I've said, or how I've apologized, you can't forgive me."

"No, I can't. Vengeance nymphs aren't very good at forgiveness. I can't forgive you any more than you can stop being what you are, Pan."

His mouth moved and she thought he was going to say something more, but he didn't. Nina hesitated at the hurt in his face. He left the bower without another word. Seconds later she heard the telltale whoosh of his transport out of the garden.

Once she knew he was gone, Nina bent over and gave in to the tears that had threatened since she'd realized what he wanted.

Pan wanted her to become his wife? It was unthinkable. When the spell ended the only thing she would have to fall back on was that she'd be able to go back to her old life without entanglements to Pan. Even now their lives weren't so closely intertwined that she couldn't go back to being simply Nemesis.

Becoming his wife only to lose him later would make her a laughingstock on Olympus. She'd lose everything, including her pride.

In all her life she'd never lost that and she wasn't going to allow it to be jeopardized now.

Nina's sobs subsided somewhat and she wiped her eyes on the sheets. Black satin sheets, the same ones she'd had in her apartment, she realized. Pan had taken over her possessions with the same passion he'd used to take over her, expecting to keep her and her things in his home.

So strange. She'd shed tears at being asked to marry. It wasn't her first offer…Earth men had occasionally grown over-fond of her and asked her to wed. She'd been flattered or had laughed at their audacity, but this was the first time she'd cried. With a start she knew that she would have been so happy at his proposal if she could have trusted it. Or trusted him.

Bitter tears mingled with her laughter. Pan honestly thought he could turn over a new leaf and become a faithful husband? It was impossible.

Nina pulled herself out of the now lonely bed and dressed. She'd hurt Pan—she knew that. Maybe this would be the final blow that ended their relationship. It was hard to see them going back to their simple cohabitation arrangement after she'd spurned his offer of marriage. But all she'd done was point out the truth. He wasn't meant for marriage any more than she was. Or, at least she wasn't meant for marriage to anyone but the one man she couldn't trust that far.

Maybe after he cooled off he'd realize she was right and they could go back to the way things had been.

For a moment she wondered where Pan had gone...probably to see Hep, she decided. That could be to the good. Maybe the goddess of love's husband could talk some sense into him. After all, he'd had plenty of experience to share about unlikely marriages. Maybe Hep could make Pan see that she was right.

Nina swallowed hard, willing herself not to cry again. She didn't want to lose Pan over this sudden wish he had to get married. They'd been getting along so well during the past six months, she'd hate to see them break up now.

Marriage. It was the best way to destroy a great relationship.

* * * * *

"Hep, how long have we been friends?"

The big god had to think about it for a moment. "I'm honestly not sure, Pan. A long time, I know." He watched Pan take a sizable sip of ale from the second mug he'd asked for since arriving uninvited at Hep's door that morning. The god had taken one look at his friend's tragic face and hauled him to his den, avoiding Aphrodite's curiosity. Whatever was going on between Pan and Nina most likely didn't need his wife's meddling.

Pan stroked his beard, staring off into space. "I was just wondering. I could be a real bastard three hundred years ago."

Hep snorted. "Three hundred years ago? Pan, I sometimes have trouble remembering a week ago. How should I know how you were like back then?"

"Nina remembers," Pan said softly. "I barely remember what came between us back then, but she does. And she hasn't forgiven me, either."

Curious in spite of himself, Hep leaned closer. "You want to talk about it?"

Pan gave a short laugh. "I might as well tell you about it. I was going to ask you to be best man."

"Best man, as in at your wedding? You and Nina getting married?" Hep beamed happily. "I'd be honored."

A wan smile crossed Pan's face. "That's excellent, I've got a best man. Now all I need is a bride."

Uh-oh. Hep patted Pan's shoulder. "She turned you down? How come?"

"She doesn't trust me. Doesn't trust that I really love her. Says it's all the spell. And some of it is my fault, because of what I did to her."

"You mean this three hundred-year ago thing? What was it?"

Pan leaned back, his face etched with pain. "That's part of the problem. I barely remember what happened. I'd met Nina and we'd hit it off really well. I'd had sex with a lot of women, but she was special. Really intense, like it was all new to her."

"New? You mean she was a virgin?"

"Nope...but she might as well have been. I don't think she'd ever had an orgasm before. We were in bed constantly, trying new things. It's been like that now, only even better." He hesitated and Hep thought he was going to say something more but Pan changed the subject instead.

"It lasted about a week, then I did something insanely stupid. I went to one of Bacchus' wine parties without her and met someone else." Pan turned a morose face to Hep. "I can't even recall her name or face, in fact I can't even remember having sex with her, but I bet Nina remembers the woman's sandal size. I tried explaining that I was hardly in possession of my faculties and that the other woman meant nothing to me but Nina was out of my life so fast I could have sworn she'd borrowed Mercury's wings."

Hep grimaced. That was a bad mistake, one of the worst a man could make. "So that's how you lost Nina last time. But things have been really good now, right? And you haven't fooled around on her."

He waited a moment and raised a quizzical eyebrow. "Have you?"

The god of the forests raised his furious head. "No, I haven't. I haven't touched another woman since Nina came back into my life!"

Pan's vehement reply reassured Hep. Maybe it wasn't too late to patch things up. Hep rather liked the idea of being a best man for his best buddy. He had a special formal toga he was dying to wear and a wedding would be a perfect venue.

Besides it would make Pan happy to marry Nina, and that's really what this was all about.

"So if you haven't given Nina any reason to doubt you, what is the problem?"

"She thinks it is all because of that wretched spell, that that's why I've been faithful to her. She believes that as soon as it ends I'll run off, chasing the next pretty woman that gives me a wink."

"She believes that, even though you've told her how much you love her?"

Pan hesitated and Hep watched as a look of wonder took over the other man's face. "I do love her, don't I? That's not infatuation, is it, Hep?"

"No, it isn't." Hep said gently. "You really do love her and that's not something that can be faked with just a spell." He thought for a moment. "At least I don't think it can, but I suspect we better ask an expert."

Before Pan could interfere, Hep strode to the door and opened it so briskly that his wife nearly fell into the room. "I think you better get in here, Appie," he said. "This is more your department than mine."

Sheepishly, the goddess Aphrodite glided gracefully into the room, her glorious complexion pinking over having been caught spying. At Pan's glare her cheeks turned a dusky rose.

"I was concerned when Pan came so early. I thought I might be of help," she tried to explain away her presence just outside the door.

"It really isn't your business, goddess."

Appie settled onto one of the smaller chairs in the room, a delicate short stool that Hep kept especially for his wife's infrequent visits to his den. She always complained about the massive size of the seating he needed, saying it made her feel unladylike to have her feet swinging off the floor.

"If it concerns you and Nina, of course it is my business. I was the one who shot you with Eros' arrow. Accidentally, of course," she added, shooting a quick glance at Hep. He shook his head over her insistence it had been an accident. He knew Appie too well to believe she hadn't somehow planned to hit both Nina and Pan.

Her current look of total innocence didn't do a thing to dissuade him of his opinion. He knew that look and it never boded well.

Appie crossed her perfect legs and smiled brightly at both of them. "So, what can I do to help?"

Rolling his eyes, Pan glared at his buddy, then shrugged like a man given no better choice. "I guess I better bring her up to speed."

Moments later Appie stared at Pan, her complexion suspiciously pale. If Hep didn't know better, he'd swear his little wife was far more disturbed by Pan's revelations than she had a right to be. In fact, she was acting downright guilty. Of what, he couldn't tell, but she sure seemed to be feeling responsible for more than just accidentally hitting someone with a bespelled arrow. At some point he was going to have to have a talk with his wife about her "little projects" as she called them. She shouldn't be interfering so much in the affairs of men or gods.

"So she refused your suit of marriage because she doesn't think she can trust that you love her? And it's because of the arrow." Aphrodite pulled a slender chain out of her pocket and played with the heart-shaped pendant it carried. "She believes that once the spell is broken you will no longer care about her, so she doesn't want to marry you."

"That's basically it," Pan said. In his face warred several emotions, anger, pride, and sorrow. Most of all Hep could see how much he really cared for his woman, even if it was inspired by a spell.

"There might be something I could do," Aphrodite said slowly. "A way to convince Nina what you feel for each other can be trusted."

To Hep's surprise, Pan slid off the chair and onto his knees in front of the goddess' chair. Limbs trembling, he stared down at the floor for an instant before seizing Appie's hand and pulling it to his lips.

"Aphrodite, please. If there is something you can do, I'd be ever in your debt." Pan's voice shook with emotion. Hep, who'd thought he knew the god well, was astonished at the depth of his friend's pain.

Appie looked distinctly uncomfortable, but she patted the back of Pan's hand and when she spoke her voice was kind. "I'll do what I can, Pan. I think I may have an argument Nina hasn't heard already." With a quick glance at Hep, she rose to her feet and headed for the door.

"Why don't you give me an hour or so and then come find us?" She nodded her head at Pan's half-empty mug of ale on the table. "You might also try and stay sober until you talk to her again. Too much ale isn't good for a relationship."

With a cheerful wave of her hand she left the room.

Hep clapped Pan on the shoulder. "Come on, buddy. The wife has one of those new espresso machines I've been eager to try out. That and some breakfast..." His voice trailed off as he ran an appraising gaze over Pan's attire.

"We might also want to fix you up a little bit. I hear women like it when a man wears something besides a loincloth. If you're going to propose to a woman, you might want to dress appropriately."

Pan laughed for the first time since arriving. "You might have a point, my friend. And a strong cup of coffee sounds pretty good right now."

Chapter Ten

Sultan: *I'll love you until the end of the Earth. You will be my morning and evening star, that which I guide my life by, and we will be together forever.*

Scheherazade: *Indeed, my lord, forever. And thus ends our story.*

Temporarily blinded by tears, Nina dashed them from her eyes before striking the period terminating the last line. She took a moment to blow her nose before typing "The End", but then she was done.

For an instant she sat in awe of what she had accomplished since Pan had left her that morning. It was like their fight had opened up a floodgate within her, and she'd known just what to write, just how the sultan and Scheherazade would have settled things between them. It was the last scene of her screenplay and the words had practically flown from her fingertips onto the screen.

She read through the scene one more time, catching what few mistakes there were before saving it onto the hard disk. She'd print it out and read it again later, before giving it to her actors to work on, but she knew it was good. No, it was better than good, it was exactly what she'd wanted it to be. And it had felt so fine to type the words "The End".

Near giddy at her accomplishment, Nina grinned to herself. She'd actually done it…she, Nina, formerly known as Nemesis, had actually finished a screenplay all by herself. Part of her realized that she'd never be the same again.

Now she was an author. The magnitude of it was enough to take her breath away. Writing had been different this time. Never before had she felt the fire of composition during creation of her screenplay. This time she'd been aflame. She couldn't type fast enough as she'd approached the final few pages.

And now it was done.

Nina closed up her machine and gave into a little victory dance around the garden. She was done, done, done! She wanted to laugh, to sing, to shout out her joy.

She wanted to drink champagne and eat rich chocolate!

No, even better. She wanted to fuck!

Some of her joy faded. Indeed, she did want to fuck. No, she wanted to make love— with Pan. Make love to him in their bed, in their bower, in their garden.

More to the point, she wanted Pan here to share her joy and take pride in her accomplishment. He'd been there for the beginning of her screenplay and had given her the tools to do it, the new computer, the inspiration, and even the statues to act it so she could work out the details in the script.

He'd been there in the beginning—he should be here now to celebrate the end. And he wasn't because of their stupid fight.

With a sigh Nina settled back onto the chair. She'd been hoping Pan would return shortly after he left, but he hadn't at all during the morning. The situation between them was as bizarre as it could get.

Pan, the consummate playboy, wanted to settle down with her and she was in love with him. His asking her to be his wife should have made her the happiest nymph on Olympus, but instead she was miserable.

For a moment she thought about reopening her computer and starting a new story, one based on her own life and Pan's. It would make a good Greek tragedy.

Trouble was she only wanted to write sensual romances, where the hero got the girl in the end and they lived happily ever after. She couldn't put her story into a book like that.

After all, she didn't anticipate a happy ending for her and Pan.

From the front of the garden a musical chime sounded, the courtesy bell she'd insisted Pan install after she'd moved in. Too many of Pan's friends had gotten into the habit of simply "dropping in" to visit him, sometime materializing at completely inopportune moments. The courtesy bell didn't stop an incoming transport but it at least warned her when she was about to get company. Sometimes there was even enough time to get her clothes back on.

A sharp breeze slipped over the garden wall and slid past Nina, catching briefly in her hair before settling into a small whirlwind in the middle of the grass. Leaves from the nearby trees and loose flower petals were caught up in the tight column of air that swirled around into the form of a slender woman. They twisted and turned and then the wind abruptly died away.

Where the whirlwind had been now stood Aphrodite, her pale blue Grecian gown immaculate, with barely a blonde hair out of place, as beautiful as ever. She turned to face Nina with a smile of amusement on her perfect lips.

Nina took one glance at the jeans and seedy T-shirt she'd thrown on that morning and it was all she could to do to avoid groaning. For a moment she wondered if she'd remembered to brush her hair. She tried running her hand through the thick strands, only to hit a snag. Nope, she hadn't.

The last person she wanted to see today was the goddess of love. The woman had been incessantly pleased by how she and Pan had taken to each other. She'd no doubt be thrilled to know that Pan had asked her to marry him, thinking that would vindicate her little trick of shooting that arrow at them.

She would not be pleased to know that Nina had refused Pan, and displeased goddesses could be unpleasant people to be around.

Very unpleasant. Nina thought about the number of people she'd seen turned into beasts or inanimate objects as a result of Aphrodite's wrath. Sometimes they were even made statues…

Nina took a quick glance over at the ones in the center of the garden. Who knew, maybe even those were people the goddess knew. But no, that couldn't be. Pan had said that he'd gotten them directly from the sculptor.

Fortunately, the goddess was still smiling as if she knew a secret joke. Surely that was a good sign. Nina had figured Pan would go to visit Hep this morning, and probably tell the god about his woes. Maybe he hadn't done so, or maybe Aphrodite hadn't been there to hear about how Nina had rejected the god's suit.

This might have nothing at all to do with Pan. Maybe there was a simple and innocent reason for the goddess visiting her this morning.

Like perhaps she wanted to borrow a cup of sugar?

Aphrodite folded her arms and gave Nina the benefit of her steady stare. Nina cringed. Somehow she didn't think the goddess was looking for sugar.

"Aphrodite, what a surprise. I'm sorry the place is such a mess..." Nina looked around and for the first time realized that there was a bit of disarray in the garden. After Pan had left that morning, she'd launched right into her screenplay, not bothering to do more than throw some clothes on and make coffee. As a result things were still scattered about from last night.

Particularly over in the bathroom area. There were melted candles and cushions over by the bathing pool, and her robe and one of Pan's loincloths lay across the bench. Nina colored as the goddess wandered over to the obvious signs of seduction, then gasped as Aphrodite picked up first her harness and then the dildo she'd worn the night before.

The goddess stared at the artificial penis and the harness with open astonishment then firmly closed her mouth and dropped both onto the cushions. She then picked up the tube of lube and stared at that for a moment. Nina began to wish that the ground beneath her would open up and she'd be plunged out of sight. If she could have transported on her own, she'd have headed for someplace else...anyplace else.

Unfortunately there was nothing she could do as Aphrodite came over to stand near her, the goddess' eyebrows still arched high from her discoveries. The perfectly shaped lips twitched with suppressed amusement and merriment danced in her eyes.

"Good morning, Nina. I'm pleased to see you looking so well. A little surprised, perhaps." She seemed to hesitate for a moment. "Hephaestus and I had a visit this morning from a most upset young god. I thought you might need a comforting shoulder as well."

Nina barely resisted a groan. As if she would ever seek comfort from Aphrodite. "I appreciate your trouble, mighty goddess, but Pan and I need to work out our own problems. You really shouldn't be so concerned."

With an infinitely graceful movement Aphrodite glided to one of the cushioned divans Nina had added to the garden to form an informal seating and conversation area. She settled herself onto the cushions, obviously making herself comfortable for an extended stay.

"Of course it is my concern, little nymph. After all, it was my accidental shooting of you with Eros' bow that caused you two to end up together. Therefore, if there are problems, I should be the one to help."

Her voice, her face, and even her posture seemed sincere. Aphrodite was determined to help and Nina knew from experience that a determined goddess was a difficult thing to get rid of. Whether or not she wanted it, she was stuck with the goddess' undesirable company for a while. She might as well make the best of it. In her rush to get to her laptop that morning she'd omitted her second daily dose of caffeine. Repressing a sigh, she headed for the kitchen. At least she could fortify herself. "Can I offer you something? Coffee, perhaps? I was just going to make some for myself."

"That would be delightful, my darling girl. And perhaps something light to nibble on? I had to leave my temple today before breakfast."

From her spot on the couch Aphrodite watched Nina turn on her espresso machine and happily took her cup when Nina returned with the finished brew and a plate of warmed cinnamon rolls.

For a moment the goddess eyed the heavy and plain mug before wiggling her fingers over it and transforming it into a delicate and elegantly decorated coffee cup, complete with saucer. Once the container met her approval she took a long appreciative sip and a bite of one of the rolls.

She smiled appreciatively. "Ah, excellent. I see you've developed some domestic skills since you've been living here."

Nina cringed but couldn't deny the goddess was right. She had become something of a homemaker through Pan's influence. More to the point, she realized that she'd learned to cook to save herself from his limited interest in the subject. Learning to make her own meals had given her more options than cold granola and herbal teas. Not that there was anything wrong with either from time to time

Nina took a big bite of her own roll. Delicious! Granola was fine, but a rich cake beat it for flavor any time. She hadn't realized how hungry she'd gotten and polished off the roll in record time, barely remembering that she had company before licking her fingers.

She had been hungrier than she thought. The food provided her a sense of strength that she knew she'd need.

The goddess cleared her throat, catching Nina's attention. Aphrodite was watching her with steady intent.

Steeling herself, Nina tried what she hoped would be a nonchalant smile. “So, you said Pan was upset. Did he explain why?”

“Oh, most certainly. He proposed marriage and you turned him down. Do I have the facts right?”

This time Nina didn’t try to conceal her sigh. “Yes. I wish he understood. It really is best for both our sakes.”

The goddess sipped more of her coffee, a bemused look on her face. “Not marrying is best for both of you? Why don’t you explain that to me?”

“We’re only together because we got shot with that arrow. The spell is bound to wear off eventually and when it does, Pan’s going to want to be free of me so he can go back to having other women.”

The goddess gave her a steady stare over the edge of her cup. “Don’t you mean that you both would want be free? Or don’t you believe you’d be interested in other men?”

No, she had no interest in other men. She was in love with Pan, and no other man appealed to her at all. But she wasn’t about to tell anyone that, least of all an interfering goddess. As far as the rest of the universe went, she was only here because of that darn spell and she’d keep her dignity when Pan finally realized he didn’t really care for her and asked her to leave.

She’d keep her dignity even if it killed her.

“My interest in men could be a factor. But it’s Pan who wants to get married.”

“Not you.” Aphrodite’s smile didn’t make Nina think that the goddess believed her. “You haven’t moved in here and made yourself at home, learned to cook, changed the way you dress, your job on Earth, and pretty much everything else about you. You haven't become the most domestic nymph I know, with or without a wedding band. Pan's dedicated himself to you. You've dedicated yourself to his lifestyle." She shook her head. "If that's not a recipe for marriage, I'm not sure what is."

Oh great gods, when put that way it did seem obvious how she felt about Pan. "It's the spell," Nina tried desperately. "That's what's making me behave like that."

"No spell can make a person change their life, Nina, at least not to this extent. You have to want to change. The same thing goes for Pan. He's changed his life around as well. He's never had a woman stay with him this long and certainly never wanted her to move in with him. Marriage is just the natural next step."

"There is nothing natural about Pan wanting to get married, Aphrodite, and you know it!" In her frustration Nina nearly shouted the words, only at the last moment remembering how picky Aphrodite was about good manners.

She groaned aloud and then inexplicably burst into tears. "Oh, why did he have to jump in front of that arrow? None of this would have happened if it hadn't been for that."

Aphrodite leaned forward, placing her cup on the small elegant table that suddenly appeared at her elbow. Even through her misery Nina noticed and admired it.

"Nina, he jumped in front of the arrow to save your life."

"That's ridiculous," she sobbed. "We barely knew each other. Why would he want to do that?"

"Well, obviously he wanted to do it because he cared about you, probably a lot more than even he knew. When he saw you in danger he couldn't help but try and rescue you."

From thin air Aphrodite pulled a pink silk handkerchief and handed it to her. "Now stop crying and blow your nose."

Nina did as she was told, noticing the lovely rose scent on the handkerchief. When the goddess of love did magic, she did it with style.

"I know that Pan was..." The goddess paused as if looking for the right words. "Well, let's just say he was easily distracted when you knew him before."

In spite of her tears, Nina almost laughed. The god had been easily distracted indeed, by anything with a pretty face, two legs, and a pussy. Or just two legs and a pussy. Or just a pussy. Or an ass...depending on how horny he'd gotten.

Aphrodite shook her head as if reading Nina's thoughts. "Yes, he was easily distracted then, but he's changed in the past three hundred years. I think he's always regretted what happened between you two and has wanted to find a way to get back together. That's why he tried to sacrifice himself to stop the arrow. Don't you think it is possible that he's used the spell as an excuse to do exactly what he's always wanted to do?"

Using the spell as an excuse to make love to her and make her his wife? Still snuffling, Nina thought about it. It really was completely absurd. Ridiculous. Insane. Except for the fact that it actually fit everything that had happened to date.

"I suppose it's possible," she allowed. "But even so, I doubt he's really sincere. I trusted him once before and it did nothing but bring me pain."

The goddess tapped her foot and nodded. "You're talking about the first time you were together. Pan wasn't ready for a full-time commitment, even if you were. Still, he didn't do the right thing."

Her head shook sadly. "How many times have I said that the worst thing anyone can do to someone they care about is betray them? It is the easiest thing to avoid, and yet it happens constantly, and the results are always catastrophic. Pan didn't want you to leave him, but he didn't think about that when he met someone who attracted him. It was the heat of the moment and he wasn't man enough to avoid the temptation."

The goddess of love's lips settled into a tight line of fury. "You were right to leave him, Nina. In fact, I don't think you should have ever taken him back."

Appalled at the Aphrodite's anger, Nina couldn't think what to do. Was Aphrodite saying she shouldn't even be with Pan now? "But I thought…you said…" She took a moment to gather her composure. "I'm only here because of the arrow you shot through us." Nina couldn't help how her voice rose under Aphrodite's furious stare. "It isn't my fault."

"Isn't it? In the past century you've done little but tease Pan with your availability…to everyone but him. Don't think he hadn't been aware of your work at the LUV channel. I bet he knew everything about you."

"He didn't know," Nina responded without thinking. "He found pictures in my apartment and was appalled…" Her voice trailed off at Aphrodite's sudden grin.

"So, the god of lust was appalled at seeing his woman in the arms of others…and yet he continues to keep her with him and even proposes marriage." A chuckle erupted from the goddess. "Sounds like love to me."

"Pan doesn't love me," Nina said but she wondered if she was right.

Aphrodite sat and recovered her cup from the small table she'd conjured to hold it. Immediately the table disappeared.

"He does love you, Nina, and you'd be a fool to believe otherwise. How else can you explain everything that's happened? It has to be more than a simple spell." She sipped the remains of her cup and shuddered.

"I hate cold espresso," she said and waved her hand with a flourish. The cup disappeared from sight.

Nina ignored the loss of her cup and considered her own problems. Pan loved her? Really loved her, not just because of a spell but because he'd cared even back then?

Aphrodite tapped her shoulder and it brought Nina back to the here and now. "I have a present for you."

"A present?" she asked.

The goddess smiled kindly. "Something I thought you should have. I meant to make it a wedding present...we can consider it an early one if you like."

Curiosity burned through Nina. What kind of gift would the goddess think she should have? "What is it?"

Aphrodite drew a thin silver chain with a single pendant, shaped like a silver heart, from a pocket. She dropped it into Nina's open palm.

"It's beautiful," Nina said, holding the gleaming object up. Simple in design, but perfectly formed, the heart seemed to call to her. With impatient fingers Nina fastened the chain around her neck, then held it up to view it more closely. "I love it, but why did you think I should have it?"

"Because the pendant is made from the arrowhead that struck you and Pan. It turned into a heart before it hit the ground."

It was the bespelled arrowhead? Nina almost pulled the cursed necklace off before she thought of how that would likely annoy Aphrodite. Better not to upset the goddess, especially when she was trying to be nice. She'd take it off later and hide it. Or, better still, maybe she'd melt it, or pound it shapeless with a hammer. That sounded like fun.

Imagining ways of destroying her gift, Nina missed it when Aphrodite rose and began to wander the garden. When Nina noticed her guest missing, she looked for her, only to discover that the goddess had paused in front of the statues of Aster and Dawn.

She leaned in to examine the pair closely. "Very nice. These must be the pair that Pygmalion made. I'd heard that Hephaestus had found a home for them." She stared closer at the molded pants on Aster and the simple gown Dawn wore. "Why are they wearing clothes?"

Hiding her smile Nina strolled over. "They were more comfortable with something on, as were Pan and myself. No point in them being naked all the time."

"Statues bothered by nudity?" Aphrodite laughed merrily. "Now I've heard everything." She darted a mischievous look at Nina. "I've heard you had them acting out scenes in your screenplay. That must have been amusing, like having your own living puppet show."

For some reason Nina felt compelled to defend her actors. “They are very good actors, Aphrodite. Some of the best I've worked with.”

“Really? I'd love to see them in action.” She waved her hand. “Could you make them perform for me?”

At least this was one way she could thwart the goddess. “No,” Nina said slowly. “I can't. I need Pan to make them come to life.”

The goddess' smile was a little too sympathetic. “Oh, you poor dear. I'm sorry, I forgot you can't do transformations.” Aphrodite pulled up her sleeves. “Don't think a thing of it, I'll do it for you.”

Before Nina could object, the goddess took a stance right in front of the statues. “*Figure of marble, figure of stone, come to life, be blood and bone.*”

Nina watched the statues came to life, the pale marble darkening to each figure's skin and hair color, his brown and black, hers tan and fiery red. Their eyes blinked and torsos stretched as first one then the other turned to gaze impassively at Nina and Aphrodite.

To Nina's surprise Aphrodite blanched, her composure seriously shaken as Aster turned his glare on her.

“You!” she said. “What are you doing here?”

Nina blinked in surprise. “You know them?”

Aphrodite turned her astonishment on her. “Don't you? This is Astraios, the Titan ruler of the stars.”

Aster grinned at her surprise but it wasn't a comforting expression. “Why, I live here, goddess. I'm a guest of Pan and Nemesis.”

“You shouldn't be in Olympus. It's forbidden!”

"Forbidden?" Dawn stepped into the conversation. "Why should Olympus be off-limits to us?"

Aphrodite's jaw dropped. "Eos, Lady of the Dawn and daughter of the Titan Hyperion? You're here as well?" She shook her head at the woman's sneering nod.

The goddess collected her scattered composure. "Olympus is forbidden to you because you are Titans. Your people sought to overthrow us and failed. That's why you're banned from here and from Earth."

"It is true we sought the overthrow of Olympus and its gods," Eos, as Nina now knew her to be, acknowledged. "But that was thousands of years ago. We grow tired of being imprisoned for ancient violations."

"Your realm isn't a prison. We gave you a world."

"Any world as small as ours and from which we can't escape is a prison, goddess," Astraios shouted. He strode forward, all male muscular power. Nina and Aphrodite fell back before his mighty rage, but he quickly took hold of them by the arms, dragging them across the grass to where Eos waited.

"What should we do with them?" he asked with a growl.

Eos folded her arms. "We should take them with us back to Titanous, I think. I know how to do a transport now, thanks to watching the Olympians, but don't have the power to get there by myself. Now, however, I can tap into Aphrodite's power..."

She stepped forward and placed her hand on Aphrodite's perfectly coiffed hair. A smile crossed her lips as a golden shimmer of power engulfed the Titan's hand. Aphrodite seemed to lose strength in her limbs. Shuddering, she leaned against Nina.

Eos raised her gleaming hands over her head. "So much power," she gloated. "Enough to do what's needed and then some. Now I can take us back to Titanous."

She touched Nina and Aphrodite and they froze into place, their bodies as still as if they were made of stone. It happened so fast that Nina's cry as she stiffened died without being heard.

Once the Olympians were secured, Astraios released them and stepped away. He turned to Eos, who seemed almost sad. She touched his shoulder. "Time to go," she told him. He nodded then grimaced as his body melted away, disappearing completely.

When he was gone, Eos turned to Nina and Aphrodite. "I'm sorry I can't take your physical frames with us, but as you will see, we have little room in Titanous. They will have to remain here, but I doubt they will come to any harm."

Laying her hands on the tops of their heads, she closed her eyes. When she opened them, figures of white marble stood before her with faces stark with fear. Eos shook her head sadly. She hadn't meant this to be quite so traumatic for them. Still, once their men arrived and saw what had happened to Aphrodite and Nemesis they would be all the more inspired to rescue them. That could prove best for her people.

Eos took a moment for a last look around the garden, breathing deeply of its perfumed air. She'd miss this place, with its living things, its tastes, smells, and other delights. She looked about for Astraios, only to remember that his statue was now gone, just as hers would be as soon as she left this plane.

She'd miss him as much as she did this world. Actually, probably more. For the first time in her life she'd been free of what she was, Eos of the dawn and daughter of Hyperion, lord of the Titans. Astraios of the stars had courted her for a long time, but she'd never been able to accept his suit. He was the Titan's captain of the guard and her father had not approved of someone so far below her in rank.

But then Astraios had volunteered for this assignment to do undercover work against the Olympians, working with her. The first time they'd made love… Eos closed her eyes remembering the feel of his hard cock shoving its way inside her, taking her maidenhood with it. He'd taken more than that as well.

Astraios held her heart as hostage as she and her father now held the Olympian women.

Shaking her head Eos moved back to where the statues were. The glow from her hands was fading and she hoped there was enough to see her back to Titanous. Placing her hands on her shoulders, she bowed her head and spoke quietly.

"Goodbye, Olympus."

Moments later there was nothing left in the garden but two marble statues of women with their eyes wide open.

Chapter Eleven

With a barely audible pop Pan materialized and stared enthusiastically around the garden. Eagerness and hope faded as he failed to find what he was looking for. "So where are they?" he demanded. "I don't see Nina or Aphrodite anywhere."

Just having finished materializing himself, Hep turned in a slow circle. He eyed the new sitting area with an approving grin. "I like what Nina's done with the place. It looks good."

"Yes, it's great," Pan said impatiently. "But what has she done with herself?" He searched the open areas of his home while Hep wandered around nodding and smiling. Other than a single empty cup in the sitting area, he saw no sign that the women had been there. He strode rapidly to the bower and threw open the door. Nope, no one here either, although he saw that the bed hadn't been made.

Grumbling, he returned to where Hep stood in the bathing area and nearly groaned aloud. The big god's gaze was fixed on several objects lying on the cushions near the pool, his eyes wide with astonishment.

Hep picked one of them up, Nina's dildo, holding it carefully by the flared end. "Is this what I think it is?"

"Never mind that now," Pan said quickly, taking it from him. He waved his hand and the dildo and other leftovers from last night's sex game disappeared, hopefully moving to their storage place in Nina's closet.

Hopefully, because Pan realized he was a little distracted and just wanted them out of sight. He hoped he didn't find the objects later in someplace even less appropriate, such as the freezer of Nina's new refrigerator. He doubted she'd be amused by his mistake and might get angry with him. Of course, before he could temper her wrath, he had to find her.

Pulling Hep away from the bath area, Pan continued to search the area for clues to his lady's whereabouts. Obviously she hadn't cleaned up since getting out of bed. Was it possible that she had been so upset that she went back to her old apartment right away?

But then there was the half-empty cup in the sitting area. Pan checked the coffeemaker in the kitchen and found the dregs of the pot still warm. Obviously Nina had been there not much more than an hour ago. That would have been about the time Aphrodite would have arrived. Pan smiled a little to himself. Having the goddess here could easily cause Nina to seek the fortification of caffeine…or even something stronger.

So it would appear that Nina had been here up to just a while ago. So, if she hadn't taken off first thing this morning and had been here when Aphrodite arrived, then where was she now? For that matter, where was the goddess who'd told them to come here? Wouldn't she have contacted them if they'd decided to go elsewhere?

"Do you think Aphrodite took her someplace?" he asked Hep, who'd now crossed the lawn to where the statues stood. The big man didn't answer, but stood staring closely at the figures with a profound frown on his face.

"Pan, get over here."

The note of urgency in the god's voice drove Pan to his side. He spared a single glance at the gleaming white figures. "What is it?"

"You notice anything strange about these statues?"

Pan gave them another look. Then another, much longer one. Instead of statues of a man and a woman, the stone figures of two women now stood on the lawn. One was dressed in a fairly typical Olympian gown, while the other wore human-styled jeans and what seemed to be a T-shirt.

Pan took a closer look at the shirt, which seemed have something written across the front in the human language, English. "'The LUV channel—as good as its name'," he read. "Hey, that's one of Nina's shirts. What's it doing on this statue?"

"That's not the interesting question, Pan," Hep said, his attention riveted to the other figure. Pan was struck by the intensity of the man's expression.

"What I want to know," Hep said, "is what my wife's face is doing on this statue!"

Shocked, Pan looked at the figure wearing Nina's shirt, only to discover that in addition to the shirt, it also wore Nina's face. He'd thought he'd been worried before but now pure terror sped through him. This was more than his lady leaving.

"Pan, can you turn them alive again?" Hep asked, a note of panic in his voice.

With a tentative hand Pan stroked the hard marble of each statue, seeking some sign of the woman's spirit. His hand lingered over Nina's perfectly shaped breast.

"I can't feel anything inside. If I made them flesh they'd be nothing more than empty shells. Whatever happened to them, their spirits are gone." Defeated, Pan's hand fell away. Their women had been turned to stone and that wasn't something they could have done on their own. Evil was at work here, and it had taken his Nina from him. It was all he could do to not to throw his arms around what was left her.

"Hep, what do you think happened?"

The god of forges continued to frown, rubbing his chin with one massive hand. "The statues you had are gone and these are left in their place. Somehow I have to say they're connected."

"You think that Dawn and Aster had something to do with this?"

"Dawn? Aster? Is that what they were called?" Pan watched fury rise in the big man as he apparently recognized the names.

Hep nodded grimly. "Now that I'm thinking about it, there was something familiar about those two." He glared at the remains of his wife. "Pan, we're going to need some supplies. We have some Titans to visit."

* * * * *

Nina tried to hug herself and failed. She simply didn't have any substance. If she looked at her arm, it appeared to be there, but she could pass it through the adjacent column without any trouble. The sensation would have made her quake with fear…if there had been anything to her to quake. As it was, she was just afraid.

Something like this had nearly happened to her sister Echo, when the spell Aphrodite had cast to make her human had failed and she'd begun to return to the spirit world. It was little comfort that Echo had won back her solid form once the man she loved, Alex, had declared his love for her. That was so unlikely to happen for her.

Thank goodness her clothes had been turned to mist as well, otherwise she might have been naked in the palace home of the Titans and that would have been embarrassing, particularly with the lascivious looks some of the Titan guards were giving her. At least she didn't have to worry about them molesting her…not much chance of that with her being unsubstantial.

As it was being little more than a free-floating spirit wasn't a lot of fun. It was hard to feel anything when you didn't have a physical skin. Besides, she wasn't sure how long she could remain as she was before dissipating.

She was glad their situation wasn't bringing her companion down. In spite of everything Aphrodite raised her golden head and glared imperiously at Hyperion, who sat on a golden throne at the end of the hallway. An old man with a long white beard, Nina could see he had strength and a strong sense of purpose. She might have held respect him but for the fact that he'd used his own daughter as bait and kidnapped them to get what he wanted.

Nina watched her companion and thought she'd never seen the goddess look—well—more like a goddess. Pride filled her at her companion's overwhelming sense of dignity.

"So you plan to keep us here? What will that buy you, Titan? What will you accomplish by holding us?"

"Your men will come looking for you and negotiate to get you free." From her position near the throne, Eos answered for her father. The Titaness was dressed in a peach-colored silken gown, fit for the princess. Her true form wasn't much different from the one she'd had as a statue, if somewhat taller.

Okay, a lot taller, like twice the size of Nina. All of the Titans lived up to their names, giants compared to the smaller Olympians. Eos could probably squash Aphrodite and Nina like bugs…if they had any substance to squash.

Near Eos stood Aster, who she now knew as Astraios, dressed as the captain of the guard. From the scowls the Titan king was giving both Eos and Astraios, he probably knew about the pair's relationship and wasn't too happy about it.

Nina wondered how that could help Aphrodite and herself, but the only thing she could think of was that if Hyperion learned that his daughter and his captain of the guard had been sexually involved because of her screenplay, she might have even less time left to exist than she did now.

Oblivious to Nina's thoughts, Eos continued on. "Once we get what we want, access to the worlds of the gods and the humans, we will give you the freedom to return to your bodies back on Olympus."

Nina shuddered at the thought of the Titans free to visit either Earth or the realm of Olympus. While she was too young to have any direct experience with them, from everything she'd heard the forerunners to the gods were uncivilized barbarians who'd nearly destroyed the world before the Olympians had locked them up for everyone's sake.

Of course, she had to admit that Dawn and Aster—that is, Eos and Astraios—had been very well behaved when they'd been in her home. If all Titans behaved the way those two did, she didn't see why they couldn't be free. After all, it had been so long ago when the Titans had ruled things and they had seemed to have learned from their mistakes. One couldn't hold the past against someone forever, particularly when they'd shown good faith in their actions.

Not unlike certain hairy-legged gods…

Nina put her hand over her mouth to keep a gasp from escaping. Unfortunately since neither her hand nor mouth was solid the gasp happened anyway and everyone in the room turned to stare at her.

She tried to shrug nonchalantly. "I just thought of something." At their continued stares, she said the first thing she could think of. "I was just wondering if I left the coffeemaker on back home."

Eos frowned, Astraios scowled, and the rest of the Titans shook their heads and turned away, but Aphrodite leaned closer. "What is it, Nina? Have you thought of a way for us to escape?"

"No, not that," she replied. It wasn't escape she was thinking of. Her thoughts about the Titans had reminded her of Pan. Wasn't it possible that if the Titans could turn over a new leaf that Pan could as well? Was she too quick to judge him based on the past when he'd given her no reason to doubt him since they'd been together?

"Aphrodite, do you think it's possible for a man to change? I mean really change?"

The goddess smiled faintly. "I see you're still thinking about Pan. Well, I want you to ask that question of yourself. Have you changed since coming to love Pan?"

"I don't love him…" she started to say, but Aphrodite's knowing smile shut her up. Nina sighed. How had she ever though she could ever hide love from the goddess who personified the subject? Talk about impossibilities.

But then there was the goddess' question to deal with. Had she changed since loving Pan, since she'd moved into his home and all but given her heart to him?

Once she'd been a real party girl, up all night, having sex with any number of men, sleeping until noon. Now she woke at dawn and was content to lie with one man alone. No one else appealed to her the way he did. Nemesis the insatiable had become Nina the content. If that wasn't a change then what could be?

Was it possible that Pan actually felt the same way, and not just because of the arrow's spell? Could it be he wanted to be only with her because they'd spent so much time together, enough time for love to grow, enough love to push out desire for anyone else?

Could Pan really love her, as he said he did, enough to change how he tended to behave?

For the first time actual hope rose in her. If her spirit had held physical form she would have still felt like floating to the ceiling. Pan loved her and she loved him. Maybe there was a possibility for a happy ending for them after all.

Then she remembered her surroundings and her greater concern returned. She and Pan might have a happy ending if she could get out of her current situation. From the grim looks of the Titans surrounding them, that seemed dubious.

"So, you think our men will bargain with you?" Aphrodite said scornfully. She floated in the air next to Nina, taking as disdainful a stance as being insubstantial allowed. "They won't, you know. They'll come in here with an army, heavily armed, and destroy you all."

Astraios sat on his big seat in the throne room, his stance as disrespectful as the goddess'. "You think so?" The big dark man flexed his muscles with an audible crack. "I'd love to see them try. It's been a long time since I've slain a god."

Nina shrank back in fear. The Olympian-Titan war had been before her time, but she'd heard the legends and knew what tough fighters the Titans were. If Pan went against them he could get hurt—or even killed!

"You don't really think our men will come and fight, do you?" she whispered to Aphrodite. "Pan isn't really a warrior."

A grimace covered Aphrodite's face and she spoke quietly so the Titans couldn't hear. "Neither is Hephaestus. I imagine they'll do something, but I doubt they'll come in here swinging swords around." She shook her head. "Of course, they will have to figure out what happened to us in the first place. They may not even notice we're gone for a while."

Aphrodite tried to lean against the wall, only to sink partway through it. Irritation showed in her face as she recovered her stance, ignoring the snickering of the watching Titans. She continued her whispered conversation with Nina.

"Knowing my husband, I'd bet he was breaking out another keg of beer for Pan, not planning a rescue."

Chapter Twelve

Pan watched Hep pull one of his kegs of special brew from the storeroom. As soon as the other god had made his announcement that they needed to "visit the Titans" he'd whisked them both back to his and Aphrodite's home. Expecting that the big god would notify the other Olympians of the Titan's treachery, Hep surprised Pan by instead spending the next half hour collecting an odd array of items, without stopping to explain anything.

Hep picked up a pair of laptops similar to Nina's as well as the keg and other items and headed towards his workshop. Pan followed him there.

"So why do you think the Titans have them?" he asked, hoping to break Hep's single-minded concentration and get some answers.

The big god paused in the middle of dragging his biggest hammer over to the pile he'd collected. "Three things. For one thing, it has been quiet in Titanous for some time now. Too quiet. Obviously they've been planning something. For another, only a Titan could pull that trick of using a god's magic against them. Someone stole Appie's power and used it to turn our women to stone and steal their spirits. Not even one of the gods could do that…but a sneaky Titan could."

Horror filled Pan. The Titans could steal a god's power? "I didn't know they could do that."

Hep pulled a net down from the wall and began bundling all his acquisitions except for the hammer in it. "It isn't widely known. Probably cause a panic in Olympus if it was. Of course not all Titans can do it…just special ones."

"Ones like those we had in our garden?" Pan thought for a moment. "Who were they, Hep?"

The big god paused in the middle of his packing. "That's the third thing that makes me think it was the Titans, who the statues were. You said one was named Aster? Was he a big muscular man, with dark skin and tightly curled black hair?"

Pan nodded. "That's him."

"Okay, that sounds like Astraios, Titan of the stars. Last I heard he was captain of the guard for Hyperion, the ruler of Titanous. Then the other's name was Dawn? I bet she was pale little thing with red hair and blue eyes."

At Pan's second nod, he grimaced. "That would be Eos, daughter of Hyperion and Titan of the dawn. It also explains why they were able to do what they did. She's one of the few Titans who can steal a god's power and that's why they were able to take Appie and Nina."

Pan looked around the workshop and saw a display of short swords on one table. Seizing one he swung it over his head. "This will do, I think." The uncommon weight of it caused him to trip and he had to catch himself before falling to the floor.

Hep looked on in thunderous disapproval. "And what do you think you're going to do with that?"

"I'm going to fight, of course." Regaining his balance, Pan turned the sword's tip towards the floor and held the pommel against his chest. "The Titans took my woman and I'm going to get her back."

Hep raised an eyebrow and leaned heavily against the workbench behind him. "You're going to take on the Titans alone, at least thirty or forty of them, all of them twice as big as you, armed with a sword you don't know how to use? I can assure you that they will have no such handicap."

"I won't be alone…you'll be there." Pan hesitated. "Won't you?" he asked plaintively. "After all, they took Appie as well…"

Pan's voice trailed off as he considered a horrible possibility. Hep and his wife didn't have the happiest of marriages, and maybe Hep wasn't all that eager to rescue her. "You do want Aphrodite back, don't you?"

Hep was in the middle of picking up what looked like a portable generator. At Pan's words, he straightened and a look of cold fury took over his features. Pan tried not to shrink from the bigger man as he hefted the apparatus in his direction. It almost looked like he intended to throw it at Pan.

Instead he took a couple of deep breaths, then placed the generator on top of the net and turned away. When he again faced Pan his expression once again held the calm control it usually had.

"Yes, I want my wife back. Believe it or not I happen to love Appie. She holds my heart and has for a long time. I keep it quiet…it doesn't always do for a man to shout out how he feels about a woman." He took a deep breath. "I don't mind telling you because I happen to know that you feel the same way about Nina."

In a move quicker than Pan would have expected, Hep took the sword from him and gave it a few practice swings. It whistled through the air with a near deafening shriek and Pan cringed at the unnatural sound. Hep grinned as he handed the weapon back to Pan.

"It's a banshee sword. Makes a sound designed to intimidate the enemy," he explained. "Take it with you it if it makes you feel better, Pan, but don't expect to use it. If it comes to fighting the battle will be lost anyway." The big god gathered the net up and slung it over his back, only staggering a little under its tremendous weight.

Hep turned to Pan. "Just remember that there is more than one way to fight a war and the best way isn't always the most obvious."

He grinned faintly. "Are you ready to deal with some Titans?"

Palms sweating, Pan clutched the pommel of his sword and held it at what he hoped was the right position. Three thousand years of existence and he'd never learned to use a sword...but there was always a first time. No one would steal his nymph and get away with it. "I'm ready, Hep."

"Good." He hefted his big hammer in his free hand, the one he used to make Zeus' thunderbolts, and lifted it high over his head. "Then let's go. As they say in the comic books, it's clobbering time!"

Pan didn't know the coordinates so he let Hep control the transport. The air shimmered around them and they disappeared from the workroom...

...only to reappear in a narrow hallway. Pan straightened then caught his breath as he looked around, gasping at the sight. Above his head was nothing but stars and between his feet—far below—he saw, floating in the midst of great open space, the realms of Earth and Olympus. It was as if the floor and ceiling were made of clear glass. Pan felt like he was floating in space. Only the narrowly spaced columns and the walls between had the look of solidity and even those were semitransparent.

A strong sense of vertigo overcame him and he pressed against the seemingly solid surface of the nearest wall until the worst of it passed. A chuckle from Hep caught his attention.

"It's pretty overwhelming at first but you'll get used to it. Just try not to look down…or up," the big god said with a wry smile. "The Olympians created Titanous as a prison, but they decided to make it as intimidating as they could. Hyperion and his family asked to be where there was light, and Zeus decided to give it to them." He indicated the lack of solid ceiling or floor. "This was the result. I helped build it, but I wasn't happy about it. I said it was a mistake to antagonize them."

Some of Pan's instinctual reaction to having the floor pulled out from under him faded away. "Zeus designed this deliberately, and then stuck the Titans here?" He shook his head. "No wonder they aren't happy with us."

"Oh, it gets worse than this," Hep replied cryptically. "But you'll no doubt see that for yourself. Right now we need to find out what's happened to our ladies. Since the Titans don't have a dungeon to stick them into, most likely they are in the throne room." He thought for a moment then nodded down the long hallway to the left. "That should be this way."

Still hefting his burden, Hep led the way down the corridor. Pan followed in his footsteps, trying to follow the god's advice not to look either up or down. As carefully as he stepped his hooves made a soft clip-clopping noise on the hard surface of the crystal clear floor.

Pan and Hep heard whispered voices approaching and hid behind a set of columns, just before the sources of the voices came into sight.

Once again Pan nearly gasped aloud, covering his mouth with his hand at the last moment. They were hidden by the columns but could still see the gigantic figures striding down the hallway from the direction they were heading. Two of the Titans passed, heavily armored and bristling with weapons.

But it wasn't their armor or weapons that surprised him. Each of the Titans was at least twice as tall as he was. Their heads barely cleared the ceiling and as Pan watched, they had to duck to pass through a doorway.

He looked back to see Hep nodding, his lips tight and expression grim. "That's what I was talking about. Not only was this place designed to have no visible ceilings or floors—they designed it for a normal-sized person. The Titans have to spend half their time ducking to avoid braining themselves."

Pan couldn't help his sigh. Not only were Nina's captors upset, they had a right to be that way. Imagine spending three thousand years in a glass box with a low ceiling. If the vertigo didn't get to you, the claustrophobia would.

Still, they shouldn't have stolen his woman from him. He wouldn't forgive them for that, no matter what their grievances, particularly if any harm had come to her. If she wasn't all right, he'd make them pay, one way or another.

Still wielding his sword, Pan silently followed Hep as they continued down the hallway.

Chapter Thirteen

Most of the Titans had gone, leaving Nina and Aphrodite to float around the throne room uncontrolled. If there was one good thing about not having a physical body, Nina decided, it was that it was really hard for anyone to physically restrain you. No locked doors or chains would hold them. The best the Titans could do was to leave someone to watch over them as the rest went about their business.

Astraios had gotten that unlucky job, sitting on one of the many benches in the throne room and glowering at them as they tried to sit as far from him as they could get. It wasn't that hard a job for him since there wasn't very much she and Aphrodite could actually do as spirits. They couldn't manipulate anything solid and even moving around the room was difficult. Moving through the air was like swimming in heavy water. After a short time neither Nina nor Aphrodite had the strength to do more than hover in one place.

It took a bit of practice to sit on a bench when gravity wasn't helping, but Aphrodite seemed to pick up the knack right away. She perched and returned Astraios' glower, her arms folded over her chest.

Nina tried to mimic her, but her forearms slid right through each other. With a sigh she left them to dangle at her side and tried to focus on something else. Her sister Echo, who'd taken the human name of Chloe, had been in almost this same situation just about half a year before.

The entirety of Chloe's left arm had been gone by the time Aphrodite had managed to reverse the spell and give her back her solidity so that she could go home to live as a human with Alex, the man she loved.

It dawned on Nina just how frightened Chloe must have been when her body had begun to evaporate. At least Nina's had gone all at once and there hadn't been the slow disintegration that Chloe had suffered.

Nina eyed the goddess carefully. She hadn't said anything, but Nina knew that she could turn a spirit solid…she'd done it with Chloe. Whispering, so their Titan guard wouldn't hear them, Nina spoke. "Aphrodite, can you reverse what Eos did to us and make us solid again?"

The goddess winced then sighed. "I could if I had any of my power left but that vixen Titaness stole it all. It will be days before I regenerate enough to make anyone solid."

Nina's heart sank. The goddess didn't have any power? Then there would be no way they could get free unless they could find another power source. Too bad she couldn't transfer some of hers to Aphrodite. She didn't have much, but…

Wait a minute. A thrill went through Nina's nearly invisible body. She *did* still have her power. She could feel it deep inside, like a tiny battery waiting to be tapped, small but ever ready. Perhaps the goddess couldn't turn them solid, but maybe she could.

"Aphrodite, could you teach me that spell?" Nina asked, still speaking quietly.

The goddess startled, then a faint smile crossed her lips. "That's not a bad idea. Could be useful if we get the chance." She held up one hand and used what little magical strength she had to read how much power Nina had. After a moment her smile faded and she shook her head sadly. Nina's heart sank.

"Good idea, but you aren't powerful enough, I'm afraid. The best you could do is turn yourself solid, and then only for a few minutes. Not long enough to escape from here." She seemed to read Nina's disappointment. "Still, who knows? Even that small amount might prove useful."

The goddess moved closer. "Here is how to do the spell," she said and proceeded to whisper the instructions into Nina's ear.

It wasn't that hard. Nina tried practicing it, turning her smallest finger solid for a few seconds then letting the spell fail and watching her hand go back to being a ghostlike, indistinct blur.

A soft sound from the other end of the throne room caught Nina's attention and she and Aphrodite turned to see the Titaness Eos enter the room. Her red hair gleamed in the constant ambient light and her eyes shimmered, but even from across the room Nina could see they shone with unshed tears and not happiness.

Astraios stood and approached her, his stance eager and hopeful. "Did you talk to him?" he asked, his rough voice softening as he spoke to her.

Eos nodded her head slowly, not meeting his eyes, and they could see the hope die in him, his hands clenching at his side. "And so," he said harshly. "What does the great Hyperion say?"

Her voice was gentle but it carried clear across the room. "He is pleased with me, and pleased with you, but…" Her words trailed off into a broken sob.

Astraios turned away, his back a solid wall of anger. One fist struck the wall in front of him, making a booming noise that startled Nina.

"But as pleased as he is, he won't agree to our being wed. I'm too far beneath you to be acceptable as his son-in-law." Nina had no trouble hearing Astraios' words as his voice rose in anger. "I risked my life in this plan of his, as did you, and our reward is to be forced apart."

She placed her hand on his shoulder, her face clouded with sorrow. "Please, Aster, give him time. He needs to see how much we mean to each other. I'm sure my father will come around in time."

He turned so suddenly her hand was thrown off. "Of course, *princess*." He said the word as if it were a curse. "I'll do anything you wish." His lips drew into a grim line. "As always."

Eos tried to reach for him again but Astraios pulled away from her and strode forcefully from the room, leaving her to collapse on a bench and burst into quiet tears as soon as he was gone.

Next to Nina, Aphrodite made a soft sound of dismay, and when Nina turned to look at her the goddess was shaking her head.

"So, there are star-crossed lovers even here." She sighed. "I can't even seem to get kidnapped without finding some kind of work to do."

Nina had to resist a chuckle. Of course Aphrodite would decide that the Titans' unfortunate love affair was hers to meddle in. After all, she'd meddled in human affairs and those of the gods. Even she and Pan were together as a result of Aphrodite's actions, although the goddess still maintained it had been an accident that she'd hit them both with Eros' arrow.

That is, she and Pan would be together if she were back on Olympus where she belonged. A sigh escaped her. She could have been in Pan's arms now if she had believed in him more this morning, if the goddess hadn't come to visit and, as a result, turned the Titans' statues to flesh.

She glanced at the heart-shaped pendant on her chest, the arrowhead that had brought Pan and her together. That too had been a result of Aphrodite's meddling, but a more positive result she couldn't imagine. Or at least it would be if she could get free and find Pan.

But there were other issues. When she did find him would she be able to touch him or would she be forced to remain a spirit from now on? Stark fear attacked again and she huddled onto the bench. Suppose she couldn't become solid again? How would she and Pan make love?

Perhaps they wouldn't be able to…but oddly enough that didn't strike her as painfully as she expected. In fact, it paled against the thought that she might not ever even see him again.

Huddling miserably on the bench, Nina missed first noticing the sound of distant shouting—men's voices and the clash of metal weapons. But she came out of her funk when it got louder and grew nearer, and Nina sat upright just as a group of several Titans came into the throne room, pushing two smaller figures before them. Behind them strode the white-bearded Hyperion, followed by Astraios, who still wore the scowl he'd had when he'd left earlier. Another Titan followed them, holding a large net packed with items, an Olympian-sized short sword and a large hammer. He piled the items in the corner of the room then left to stand with the others.

Nina gasped as the figures were revealed to be Hep and Pan, their arms tied behind their backs. Both men looked only somewhat disheveled, as if they had been captured without much of a battle. Nina breathed a sigh of relief when she realized neither man seemed hurt.

Aphrodite made a sound of disgust and rolled her eyes. "Well, this is quite a rescue," she said quietly to Nina. "They got here only to get themselves captured."

"Maybe they told Zeus and the others what had happened to us," Nina said hopefully. "Surely they didn't just come here without backup."

"I wouldn't put it past Hephaestus to do exactly that. He's always said we should try and make peace with the Titans." She nodded at the pile of items in the corner. "Knowing him he probably intended to talk them out of holding us."

Nina could see Pan's gaze darting about, probably looking for her. She knew when he saw her…first his face brightened but then he paled when he realized he could see right through her. Finally, his gaze grew hot with anger and he struggled fruitlessly against the ropes holding him. One of the Titans reached over to catch hold of him and he spun away from the big hand.

"Let me go. I just want to talk to my wife."

"Wife?" Hyperion laughed wickedly. "I wasn't aware you were married, little god." He grinned at Nina. "In fact, I seem to remember hearing that she'd turned you down."

Nina looked at the clear floor and realized she could see all the way to Olympus. If she looked carefully she could even see Pan's garden home. Hyperion, from his all-seeing throne, could probably see a whole lot more. He'd been spying on them all this time! Her cheeks burned when she remembered just what he might have seen her and Pan doing. Thank goodness there was a cover over the bathing pool where they'd made love the night before!

She raised her head and glared at the Titan king. "So you've been watching us. I suppose you've seen your daughter and Astraios as well."

Now it was Hyperion's turn to look angry. "They did what they did to help our people get free of this prison the Olympians made for us. We're all tired of living in a glass box."

"It wasn't just to help your people, Hyperion," Aphrodite interjected. "They love each other and you're wrong to keep them apart."

With a growl, Hyperion turned to sneer at her. "You mind your own business, goddess. It's bad enough you get involved in other people's love lives—you leave ours alone."

"But I'm the goddess of love…it's my job," she said indignantly.

"Not around here." He returned his attention to the bound gods. While Pan still struggled to be free, Hep stood patiently, apparently unconcerned by being outnumbered, outweighed, tied up and disarmed. Nina hoped he had some sort of plan to support his attitude of calm.

Hyperion leaned over them. "So, little gods, to what do I owe the honor of this visit?"

Hep shrugged. "We were just in the neighborhood. Thought we'd stop in. Maybe do some trading."

The Titan smiled, the expression almost looking genuine. "You have something to trade in equal value to a pair of goddesses…" He made a withering glance at Nina.

"Well, all right, one goddess and one little nymph," he shrugged. "Not worth that much, I suppose."

Nina could feel Pan seethe over the slight to her and she wasn't that far from seething herself. The nerve Hyperion had. Just because he was bigger, stronger, and in charge didn't permit the Titan to be insulting. Well, she amended, maybe it did give him the ability, but it shouldn't. He was just being a big bully.

"Still," Hyperion continued. "They mean something to you two, otherwise you wouldn't have come for them."

"Yes, they mean much to us." Hep continued to face the Titan as if his hands weren't tied behind his back, leveling a steady gaze at those in the room around him. The big god's calm presence steadied Nina, who wasn't feeling all that composed at the moment. All she had to do was glance at Pan, still struggling against his bonds, and fury filled her.

Hep nodded to Nina and Aphrodite. "You've gotten our attention, Hyperion, and we will negotiate with you, but first I want you to release the women and send them back to their bodies. Stealing them was wrong and against all the rules. We don't make war this way, through the kidnapping of the weak."

Nina narrowed her eyes at Hep. Now she had a new target for her irritation. "Who's he calling weak?" she muttered. "I'm no shrinking violet. I was a vengeance nymph for a long time before I got into the sex film business."

That thought gave her an idea and she took another glance at the items piled over in the corner. There was a short sword that she recognized as a banshee sword. Once upon a time she'd been pretty good with one of those. Quietly Nina began to formulate a plan.

Hyperion strode within a foot of Hephaestus and stared down at him. Pan quit fighting his bonds and stepped closer to his friend, his face showing the same determination as Hep's.

The Titan took no notice. "You're in no position to bargain, little god. I want freedom for my people, all of those here. We've been held in this place too long."

"I agree with that, but this is the wrong way to go about getting it," Hep replied. "You should have petitioned Olympus..."

Hyperion swept a hand about, inches above Hep and Pan's heads. Again Nina watched in amazement as neither god ducked, Pan's hair ruffling under the wind created by the Titan's near blow. Her admiration for both of them rose.

"I did petition Olympus, but they wouldn't listen. They said I'd need an advocate to make my case."

Hep nodded. "Very well. Once you release the women I'll agree to be your advocate. I'm sure in a few weeks we'll be able to do something..."

"No!" Hyperion roared, his face contorted with fury. "Not in a few weeks, not even in a few days. We want our freedom now!"

Hephaestus continued calmly, as if the Titan hadn't interrupted him. "...we'll need to document how much you've learned since being here. You will need to prove you can be upstanding citizens, will do good works on Olympus and will be able to visit Earth without revealing what you are. There are rules you know."

"I'm king of the Titans, little god. I make the rules, I don't have to follow them!"

"And that's precisely why you were stuck here in the first place." Hep shook his head sadly. "I'd hoped you'd learned something by now, but perhaps I was wrong. You must be able to fit into the worlds of others if you want to live there."

"Father," Eos broke in, her face troubled. "Perhaps the god is right. The benefits of freedom would more than make up for obeying a few rules. If we could win our release through negotiation there could be a lasting peace between our people. Otherwise there will be fighting and we could end up back here…or someplace even worse."

Nina saw some of the other Titans nodding their agreement with Eos. Astraios frowned, but he seemed to be considering the wisdom of her words.

Only Hyperion glared at his daughter. "We hold these women whom these gods find precious. Why should we negotiate with them when we can simply take what we want?"

"Because it's wrong to use force to take what one wants, Father. The god offers to help us, why not allow him to do so, without using force?"

Aphrodite leaned into Nina and whispered. "I like this Titaness more all the time. I think she should be united with the man she loves." She turned her speculative stare on Astraios, who watched Eos with undisguised admiration and desire. Nina smothered a grin. Even reduced to a spirit state without any of her divine powers the goddess couldn't help her inclination to play matchmaker.

"You must release Nina and Aphrodite, Hyperion," Pan said. "Then we'll help make your case to the Olympian court."

Hyperion leaned over Pan. "You should be careful who you order around, god of the forests and fields." He placed his hands on either side of Pan's head. "You're in my control now. I could easily steal your power and use it to break free from this prison."

Immediately Nina was on her feet and gliding towards them. Hyperion spared her a quick glance and then laughed. "So, the little nymph thinks to get involved." He struck at her with a heavy hand before Nina could duck away from him. Those in the room gasped, first in horror, then in relief his hand passed completely though her body without harm.

Nina felt relief as well. One thing about being disembodied—she had no body to be hurt. Still, she slid away from him as if frightened by what his hand had done to her, making sure her path took her closer to the pile of Olympian objects in the corner.

"You had no call to do that, Hyperion," Pan said, his face furious. "She's defenseless and has done nothing to you. She wasn't even born when you were imprisoned here."

Even Hyperion looked uncomfortable. "I don't think I hurt her." He looked around to see where she'd gotten to but Nina ducked behind the throne where he couldn't see her. Shaking his head, he returned his attention to Pan. "She shouldn't have interfered. No one should defy me. I'm the one in power here."

"And that's why you will always lose in the end, Hyperion," Pan said. "You're a bully and as soon as a bigger bully comes along you'll not have anyone to help you."

Nina crept closer to the short sword, keeping an eye on where Eos stood on the steps next to the throne. She had a plan, but she would have to act fast. No one was paying attention to her anymore, instead watching the confrontation between Pan and Hyperion. This was the chance she'd been looking for.

Experimentally, she turned her hand solid again and reached for the hilt of the sword. It felt cool and comforting against her palm, but without the rest of her arm she wouldn't be able to lift it.

Aphrodite had said she would only have the power to turn solid for a short time. Nina hoped it would be long enough. In her mind Nina spoke the spell, tapping into the last of her power as she did so. Big magic was hard for her and she struggled to control the flow, but she felt herself turn heavy in Titanous' normal gravity as her body solidified. As quietly as possible she lifted the sword from the floor, the hilt a familiar presence in her hand.

Nina smiled. Once a vengeance nymph, always a vengeance nymph.

She took a deep breath, preparing for the next step and pleased to feel her lungs expand. Now where was Eos?

Standing by herself, right by the steps to the throne, a perfect location. While everyone watched the Titan king arguing with the gods in the middle of the room, Nina dashed up the steps and behind the Titaness. The steps put her in the right position to throw one arm around Eos' throat.

She swung the sword hard and it made a deafening scream, drowning out Eos' cry. Everyone covered his or her ears from the eerie sound. Seconds later Nina had the sword's edge against the Titan's pulse. All those in the room turned to face her.

The larger woman's hands tried to dislodge Nina's arm, but she held on fast. She poured whatever power she had left into the strength of her arm, anger and determination boosting it. Meanwhile, she held the sword's edge against Eos' neck, letting the blade catch the light to bounce it around the room so everyone saw it. Eos felt its sharp edge and froze in place, as did everyone else.

Astraios took two steps towards them before immobilizing as well, his sword held high. He stood so still, Nina could almost believe he'd returned to stone. Only the clenching and unclenching of his fist and the way his dark skin beaded with sweat told her he was still a living and breathing man.

"Now," Nina said, letting all her fury at the Titans show in her voice. "You'll disarm yourselves and release Pan and Hephaestus. Do it now or she dies."

"You wouldn't dare…" Hyperion said, his face paling at the threat to his daughter.

"Don't believe that for a moment. You forget, Titan, that this nymph's real name is Nemesis, former vengeance nymph, and that I am well practiced at using a sword to kill. It's been a long time," she admitted with a fierce grin, "but I think it will come back to me."

As they hesitated she let the blade's edge slide deeper against the Titaness' skin, not breaking it, but enough to hurt. Eos' eyes grew wide.

Pulling a wickedly sharp-looking knife, Hyperion grabbed Pan and held the knife to his chest. "Hurt my daughter and I'll take some vengeance myself." He glared at Nina. "I don't think you want him dead."

The sword trembled in Nina's hand, but she held firm. "You'd sacrifice your daughter?"

"Would you sacrifice your lover?"

*A vengeance nymph would...*Nina thought. That's who she was supposed to be—a woman incapable of love and unable to forgive...except that wasn't who she was anymore. She loved Pan and seeing him in danger nothing mattered but his safety. Not who she was supposed to be, her attempt to free them from the Titans, and not anything from either of their pasts.

All that was important was that her lover had a knife pointed at his heart. There was no way she could let Hyperion harm Pan. She took a deep breath and prepared to release Eos.

"Hold!" A new man's voice rang through the sharp silence and Nina glanced over to see a golden-haired Titan stride briskly into the throne room. His heated stare took in all of them, including Nina with her sword at Eos' throat, but he saved his fiercest glare for Hyperion. "This has gone far enough. The past holds enough bloodshed...we have no need for more now."

"Who are you to give orders?" Hyperion growled. "Go back to your studies, Helios, this is man's work."

The Titan of the sun didn't back down. "This is work for a leader, Father, something you've obviously forgotten how to be. A leader uses words, not weapons when dealing with others. You've become too isolated...you see everything but understand little. Kill these gods or their women, and the Olympians will hunt us to extinction."

He glanced over at Astraios and the other Titans. "Our ideas are as confined as the box we live in. We need to learn new ways if we want to live outside of it."

"What new ways?" Astraios stepped forward, his sword dipping towards the floor. Nina saw how eager he was for a solution that didn't mean Eos' death. "What would you have us do?" His voice trailed off as he noted the fury on Hyperion's face.

Helios ignored his father's wrath. "For some time I've exchanged messages with certain Olympians about negotiating a new treaty, one that would get us free of here. Your actions and Hyperion's have jeopardized that. To fix things we need a show of good faith. We can start by releasing these people." He waved his hands at the other Titans in the room. "Drop your weapons."

The dark-skinned Titan nodded, then with a sharp clang, Astraios' sword hit the floor. "All of you, disarm," he told his men. "We won't allow our princess to come to harm."

"No!" Hyperion shouted, recovering his bluster. "We won't surrender. Better she die than we be kept here any longer."

Astraios glared at him. "You would risk your daughter's life? That isn't acceptable, Hyperion. We shouldn't have stolen the women's spirits in the first place. Like Helios said, we should have asked the Olympians for an advocate and a hearing on our fitness to live outside of Titanous. By our actions we've shown how unfit we really are."

He turned a troubled stare at Eos with Nina's sword at her throat. "I would rather live in a glass box the rest of my days than see you come to harm, my princess." One hand waved at the rest of the guards still holding their weapons. "I said disarm!"

There was a fierce clatter as the other Titans hurried to obey their captain. Helios strode towards his father, who still held the knife on Pan. "Let him go, Father. We can't win our freedom by hurting others."

Hyperion stared at his son, then at Nina, still holding her sword on Eos. He took a long look at the other Titans, now disarmed and staring at him.

"You've turned them all against me," he said. "I hope you know what you've done. We'll be confined here forever."

"I know what I'm doing, Father. This isn't the way." Helios took hold of the knife and after a brief struggle Hyperion let him have it. Stepping back, he watched as Helios cut free the gods. Pan gathered the swords and threw them to the side while Aphrodite rushed over to Hep to throw her arms around him.

"My hero," she cried, even as her arms failed to take hold of him and passed through his body.

Hep chuckled in his deep voice and reached out to gently stroke the space where her face should be. "Hold that thought, Appie. We'll get back to it later." He looked over at Nina. "You can let her go now."

"As you say, Hep." Nina released Eos, who quickly stepped into the waiting arms of Astraios. With relief she noted only the faintest red mark where the sword had been held on the Titaness' throat. Nina smiled at the blade her hand. At least she hadn't lost her touch with one of these.

Unfortunately, it was getting very heavy and Nina let it fall to her side then clatter to the floor. Her whole body seemed to shiver as the spell she'd used to turn solid finally ran out of power. Nina collapsed onto the throne room steps and tried to control her fear as the spell failed and she was left immaterial once again.

Pan noticed and ran to her side. He tried to brush the hair from her forehead only to have his hand pass through her head.

Once he got over his surprise, amusement took over his face. "You knew you could only turn solid for a short time?" he whispered. At Nina's nod, he grinned. "Nice bluff, vengeance nymph. I'll have to avoid playing card games with you."

In spite of her exhaustion she managed a wicked smile. "What about a game of strip poker?"

He snickered. "Now that has possibilities."

They both turned to watch Hyperion, who stood looking defeated.

"So what are you doing waiting around?" Hyperion said to Hephaestus. "You've got what you came for. You know how to return to Olympus and take the women's spirits with you."

Hep nodded. "Yes, we know, but we haven't finished our business yet, Titan."

"It isn't enough that you'd defeated us? Do you intend revenge as well?"

Ignoring the Titan king's comment, Hep folded his arms and regarded Helios carefully. "What are your intentions?" he asked the golden-haired Titan.

"As we discussed, I want what's best for my people. I want their freedom, to live where they want—and love whomever they want." He threw a quick glance at Eos, cradled in Astraios' arms. "We've been confined long enough."

"Do you want to be their ruler?"

"Ruler?" Helios gave a short laugh. "If needed I'd lead them, but I have no desire to be their king." He threw a short glance at his father. "We already have one of those."

Hyperion stared at him. "You don't want to be king?"

He shook his head. "No, Father. I want our freedom and peace for all, and I want you to listen to me once in a while, but you can keep your throne." He glanced over at Eos and Astraios. "Of course you've also got to be ready to accept new ideas…such as giving your people choices."

The wily old king seemed to consider his son's words. "You want to advise me?"

"If you will promise to listen to my advice."

For a long moment father and son stared at each other. Finally the old man nodded. "Very well, from now on you're my chancellor and I will hear your new ways." He gave a hard look at Eos and Astraios. "Even the ones I don't like."

Hep settled onto a bench. "Very well, now that we've settled who is in charge, we can return to our previous discussion. You want your freedom to visit Olympus and to explore the world of men. To gain that you need an advocate to address the Olympian court of justice," he hesitated and looked around. "Anyone here mind if I take that job?"

Smiling, Helios said nothing, but the rest of the Titans stared at the god in disbelief.

At their shocked silence Hep nodded with satisfaction. "I'll take that as a yes. So, as your advocate I'll need you to document how you've changed and what you intend to do with your freedom. You'll have to be able to pass the Earth-bound transport test…"

They continued to look blankly at them, so Hep explained further. "It's a set of questions that show you know how to deal with the normal humans on Earth without causing trouble. Not hard to pass if you do a bit of studying."

Still holding Eos close to him, Astraios was the first to speak. "You are still willing to help us, Hephaestus?"

"I came here willing to help you. If you'd asked me, I'd have come sooner."

Finally Helios broke his silence and turned to face the rest of the Titans. "I vote we make Hephaestus our advocate on Olympus. All in favor?"

There were a number of ayes as well as some comments in agreement. Even Hyperion nodded reluctantly. Helios went on. "Very well, we're agreed. Astraios, Eos, I suggest you be the ones to work directly with the Olympians." He gave a glance at Eos, who still stood in circle of the dark Titan's arms. "You two spent time there and know them better than the rest of us."

General approval broke out at that. Only Hyperion continued to glare, disgruntled, at the young couple.

Hep nodded his approval. "Very well, I'll talk to the Olympian court for you. And call me Hep, most of my friends do."

The Titan stuck out his hand. "Very well, call me Aster." He gave Eos a smile. "It's a name given me by a very special friend. But how are we going to do all this, the documenting and studying."

Hep rubbed his hands. "Ah, I was just getting to that. Someone want to bring me my bundle?"

He opened the net, pulled out a pair of laptops similar to Nina's, and handed one to Helios and the other to Eos. "These are to connect you to the Olympian intranet and Earth's Internet. You can find almost anything you want to know using those, including the answers to your questions. I've already set them up with web browsers and bookmarks so you can find stuff. Plus you can use the word processor programs to prepare your documentation for the hearings. This is for power," he said, pulling out the portable generator.

Helios' eyes lit up at the machine in his hands, opening it up and running appreciative hands over the keyboard. Nina thought he looked like a kid at holiday time. "Oh, we will make excellent use of these."

"And what about this," Astraios said, pulling the keg from the net.

Aphrodite rolled her eyes at Nina. "See, I told you beer would be involved."

Hep took it from him with a big grin. "That is some of my most special brew to celebrate our agreement. But before we open that up I have one more thing to do."

Recovering his hammer, Hep strode to the throne and stood on it, raising the hammer over his head. "I've been wanting to do this for a long time."

As the obvious target, Hyperion winced, then stood firm. He lifted his white-haired head and stared at the god and his mighty weapon. "Go ahead, I deserve it."

Appalled, Helios stepped between them. "No, Hep. No bloodshed!"

Hep's lips twitched in amusement. "Don't worry, Helios, your father isn't what I planned to hit when I brought this." Instead of throwing the hammer, he aimed it at the glass above the throne and gave it a fierce blow. The entire ceiling of the room cracked and shattered into tiny fragments that drifted slowly and harmlessly to the floor, leaving the Titans' throne room open to the universe above.

A shout started up among the Titans as, for the first time in thousands of years, they could stretch their arms over their heads and not hit the ceiling of a room. They jumped up and down and cheered, clapping Hep's back as he moved through them back to where Nina, Pan and Aphrodite waited.

"I never could stand glass ceilings," he told them. "There's just something not right about them."

Pan tried to put his arm around Nina and failed. "Hep, I think it's time to go now." He nodded at the happy Titans, now passing around glasses of Hephaestus' special brew and celebrating. Even Hyperion, who'd reclaimed his seat on the throne, lifted his glass at them. He gave a hint of a frown when Eos and Astraios threw their arms around each other and kissed, then shrugged and drank more of his beer as Helios, now the Titans' chancellor, sat next to him with the open laptop and demonstrated how it worked.

Aphrodite smiled. "Well, maybe the old man won't need a lesson in not standing in love's way after all." She glanced down at her vaporous body. "Speaking of love," she said seductively, "I'd like to return to my physical self, if you don't mind." She pretended to run a finger up her husband's chest. "I want to thank you for your rescue properly, with a kiss. And other things," she said suggestively.

Hep's eyes lit up and he nodded. "Yeah, it's time to go."

They waved goodbye at the celebrating Titans then Hep spoke the spell that returned them to Olympus.

* * * * *

They returned to the garden, the men in their normal forms, the women back into their bodies, still frozen as statues. Pan touched Aphrodite's figure at once and she turned to flesh, falling into Hep's open arms.

"My hero," she cooed, repeating her words from the throne room.

Holding her close, Hep grinned at her. "Let's go home, Appie." In the blink of an eye they were gone.

Pan turned to Nina's statue. He crossed his arms deliberately, keeping his hands well away from her. "Okay, let's talk again about marriage."

From the statue came Nina's disembodied voice. "Pan, aren't you going to return me to normal?"

The god's mouth twitched mischievously. "Not just yet. I want to make sure you hear what I have to say and this way I know I have your complete attention."

"But Pan," Nina said plaintively. "This isn't all that comfortable. I have an itch..."

His amusement deepened. "And I'd love to scratch it, but that will have to wait for later. I know that desiring you is part of the arrow's spell, but that's not the only thing you and I have going on. We both know there is more than just sex between us. You and I, we have something special." He hesitated, but decided that since it had come up already he might as well address the subject directly.

"The truth is, we always did. I fell for you pretty hard back when we were first together. I think it may have scared me a little at the time and I wasn't prepared for it. So… I did something stupid just to prove I wasn't as stuck on you as I seemed to be. When I got drunk at Baccus' party and this woman made a play for me, I went along with it. After all, that's who I was supposed to be, the god of sensual pleasure." He shook his head. "If it makes any difference to you I was so drunk that night I don't remember a thing about what happened. Later I wanted to explain and ask you to forgive me…"

A harsh laugh came from the statue. "You were going to ask forgiveness from a vengeance nymph? What would you have expected to happen? I had to be true to my nature as well."

He raised his head proudly. "Well, I'm not the same god I was back then. You don't want to be my wife because you're afraid I'll hurt you again, but I won't. I'm not like that anymore. I love you and I'd never hurt someone I love. If you'd dare to admit it, you aren't the same either. I think you can forgive me now for what I did in the long-ago past, particularly since I'm promising to never do it again."

Pan took a deep breath. "So I'm asking you again, Nina. Be my wife?"

She was quiet so long, he wondered if he'd gone too far, or if her spirit had somehow managed to leave the shelter of the stone figure. Then she spoke, quietly. "Will you set me free so I can give you my answer?"

For a moment he thought of refusing. She couldn't leave him if she was stone and if the answer was no he could continue to argue with her. But keeping her prisoner until she agreed with him? Tempting as it was, that would be wrong.

He passed his hand over her face. "*Come to life and be my love, sweet Nina.*"

The stone shimmered with color and softened, and again Nina stood in the garden. At her frown, Pan's heart sank, but he steeled himself for her answer.

"That wasn't very nice, leaving me a statue like that," she said.

So it was going to be like that. Pan sighed and nodded. "I'm sorry. It won't happen again."

A slight smile crossed her face. "Very well. I forgive you."

For a moment he was struck dumb. Then, as he realized what she'd said, the joy in him tore a shout from his lips. "You *forgive* me?"

Now Nina was grinning. "Yes, I forgive you. For everything just in case that wasn't clear." She gave a pensive sigh. "You say you've changed…well, so have I. I was going to let Eos free before Helios showed up. I couldn't let Hyperion hurt you. I guess I'm not much of a vengeance nymph anymore."

"As long as you're my loving little nymph, you can be anything you want, Nina." His heart lightened. "So you'll marry me?"

She slid into his arms. "Yes, I'll marry you. As soon as we can make the arrangements."

Some of Pan's happiness faded. "Arrangements?"

Apparently oblivious to his growing dismay, Nina began to enumerate on her fingers. "For a wedding we'll need to make a guest list and find a date everyone can come." She looked around the quiet intimacy of their garden. "We can have the ceremony here, but will need extra furniture for the party afterward. Zeus can officiate, of course."

She eyed his outfit, the tan slacks and polo shirt that Hep had talked him into this morning, saying that when a man was proposing marriage he wanted to look his best. Pan thought he looked best in a loincloth, but who was he to argue with a married man?

He remembered how Aphrodite and Hep had looked while leaving and added, a *happily* married man.

"Not bad," Nina said approvingly, and Pan preened. Hep did know what he was talking about. She grinned at him. "I can't wait to see you in a tux."

A tux? Dumbfounded, Pan watched Nina head for her computer.

"There is so much to do. We should get started right away."

"Wait just a minute!" Pan bellowed, striding after her.

Nina turned. "What is it?"

He stared down at her. "Planning a wedding is not how I want to spend the rest of this afternoon."

"Oh?" she glared up at him, but Pan could see how she was teasing him. "And what makes you think what you want means anything?"

His eyes narrowed. "You are STILL the mouthiest little nymph I know. And there is only one cure for that."

She stepped closer, clear mischief on her mind. "Oh, what's that?"

"This." Seizing her by the shoulders, Pan pulled her into a kiss. Not just any kiss, but a kiss that set all records for heat generated by single meeting of lips. As always, he felt her melt, her legs going limp as he broke it off and she swooned into his arms.

Ah, yes. That was more like it.

He lifted her over his shoulder and headed for the bower. Just before they reached the door, Nina recovered enough to laugh. "I've always loved this part, Pan."

He grinned. "I know. That's why I do it."

Chapter Fourteen

It took two months to work out the plans for their wedding, but when the time finally came Nina decided that the result was worth the wait. The day dawned beautifully, as was typical for Olympus, warm but not too warm, just perfect for the off-the-shoulder Grecian wedding gown she'd picked out.

Pan was a little less comfortable in his tuxedo, and he'd managed to misplace the tie that went with it, but he still was the handsomest man in the garden. He'd polished his hooves so they gleamed against the grass and she barely even noticed the absence of shoes.

Hep stood proudly by as best man, wearing a superb new toga that had all the women eyeing him, although none more than his wife, Aphrodite. Nina had brought Echo—that is, Chloe—and her fiancé Alex to Olympus to be her maid of honor. It was amusing watching the human man trying not to stare at all the mythical people and creatures around him.

The ceremony was brief but moving, with Zeus nodding wisely as she and Pan exchanged vows. She was surprised when Pan produced a ring for her, since that was rarely done on Olympus, but was pleased by his explanation that this way all the humans she worked with would know she was spoken for.

That wasn't even an issue. When she'd returned to the LUV channel with her Arabian Nights script, everyone had congratulated her, telling her that the glow on her face meant she was either pregnant or deeply in love.

When Pan took her hand after their vows and slipped the narrow gold band onto her finger, she knew that they were at least half right. She was deeply in love with her husband, hairy legs and all.

Now that the ceremony was over, the party was in real swing. Nina smiled at her new husband as he passed around glasses of Hep's beer, much to everyone's pleasure, especially the Titans, who'd developed a real taste for the brew.

Alex tried it and complimented the weaponsmith on his creation. A single affectionate blow from Hep's hand almost landed her sister's husband-to-be in the fish pond, but Pan grabbed the man's belt at the last moment and pulled him to safety.

Now the three of them were drinking, laughing and joking in the corner. Nina was watching them from a distance when a beautiful young woman approached. She smiled tentatively and put out her hand.

"Nemesis, I wanted to thank you for inviting me."

"Call me, Nina, please," she said, taking the proffered hand and trying to place who the woman was. Finally she shook her head. "I'm sorry, there were so many people invited. I don't remember your name."

A wry smile appeared on the other's face. "I'm not surprised. It was so long ago we met. About three hundred years." She hesitated. "I'm Livinia."

"Livinia..." Nina's voice trailed off as she placed the name and her cordial mood disintegrated. This was the former vestal virgin who'd seduced Pan so long ago, ruining her chance at happiness with him at that distant time.

Nina struggled to control her anger. She'd forgiven Pan already. She could do the same with this person. After all, she wasn't a vengeance nymph anymore…

"I see you remember me," the other woman said quietly. "I don't blame you for being upset. What I did was wrong, trying to steal your man from you." She tried what seemed like a sincere smile. "I'm just so glad it worked out for you after all this time."

Nina took a deep breath. The woman was being nice. She in turn would be polite. She would be a good hostess. She would not rip the hair from Livinia's head.

Realizing she was still tightly gripping the other woman's hand, Nina dropped it and tried not to feel pleased when Livinia rubbed it, obviously trying to return circulation to her fingers. She tried a smile that didn't go further than her teeth.

Polite conversation was called for. Something noncontroversial. "So, Livinia, tell me about yourself. What do you do now?"

"Oh, I'm still a vestal virgin," she said, pointing to her outfit, which Nina now recognized as the official VV formal gown.

For a moment Nina didn't think she'd heard right. "Isn't that a bit tricky? After all, you have spent the night with Pan."

Livinia blinked at her, then her eyes widened and jaw dropped. I'm afraid you have the wrong idea, Nina. I said I *tried* to steal your man, I didn't say I was successful."

Her laugh was rueful. "He was pretty much the worse for wine, but all he could do was talk about how much he loved you. I decided if I was going to give up my virginity it would have to be to a man who cared for me the way he did you." Again she laughed and pointed to her gown. "As you can see I'm still looking."

Stunned, Nina exchanged further pleasantries with Livinia but couldn't remember later what they talked about. As she watched the woman walk off, she considered what she now knew. Pan hadn't been unfaithful to her all those long years ago. More to the point, if either of them had looked beyond their own concerns they would have known he hadn't been since Livinia was still a virgin. All this time this time they'd been apart because neither of them had faced the situation honestly.

Honesty and trust. Nina vowed that from now on that's what she and Pan were going to have in their relationship.

For a moment she considered telling Pan what she'd learned, but decided to keep it for later. Instead she moved closer to where the men were talking. From what she could hear the two gods were teasing Alex about his impending plunge into wedded bliss. Pan looked over to grin at her and she grinned back.

Her face exhibiting exasperation, Chloe came over to stand with Nina. She nodded at the cluster of men. "I swear, if they talk Alex out of it, I'll turn vengeance nymph and take them all on."

"No fear of that," a soft voice interrupted and they turned to see Eros approach. "I can see from their smiles how much your men love you. They tease, but they are happy to have you."

The god of love resembled his name. Soft golden curls covered his head and his smile was so sweet he looked as innocent as a young child.

Nina tried to control her snicker at that thought. She'd once been in Eros' bedroom and found his and his loving wife's closet of sex toys. Innocent was one thing he wasn't. He glanced at her and the twinkle in his eyes made her wonder if he could read her thoughts. Oh, well, who wouldn't be thinking about sex when they were married to Pan, a god who lived up to his reputation for sensuality.

Eros reached over and touched the heart pendant she was wearing. A grin took over his face. "Where did you get this? It looks like one of my arrowheads."

Well, she'd hoped to avoid ever telling him, but it was such a special day. Nina couldn't seem to tell any lies today. "Actually, it is." She took a deep breath. "Aphrodite gave it to me. It seemed appropriate to wear today because it's from the arrow that struck me and Pan and brought us together."

Confusion and concern showed in Eros' eyes. "I never shot you with an arrow Nina, nor Pan."

"It wasn't you that fired it," she said. For a moment Nina felt like melting into the ground. "Aphrodite did it. She was angry with me for interfering with her plans for Chloe and Alex."

"Nina was trying to help me," Chloe burst in. "So she had one of your bows and an arrow."

Eros stared. "You took one of my bows and arrows?"

"I know it was wrong, but Chloe was so unhappy and was going to have to turn back into a statue, and I thought if I could just make Alex love her everything would be all right." Words of explanation poured out of Nina's mouth at the god's censuring look.

Chloe put her arm around Nina's shoulders. "She really only wanted to make Alex love me."

"I'm so sorry, Eros. I really am," Nina said mournfully.

Their words must have touched his heart because Eros shook his head. "You meant well, I guess, and as it turned out no harm was done."

His serious look faded and he burst into a grin. "It's a good thing it was only a practice arrow."

It took a moment for his words to make sense. Nina shook her head. "What do you mean it was a practice arrow?"

"Just that. It was from my smallest bow set, right? The wooden one? That's left over from when I was just a little god. Mom didn't trust me with a bespelled set so she gave me the wooden one to practice with."

Nina grew cold inside. "Aphrodite knew it was a practice set?"

Their conversation had gotten louder and attracted the attention of the men. Pan was suddenly by Nina's side, listening closely to Eros' words. "Let me get this straight, Eros. It was a practice bow and one of its arrows that Nina took? There was no spell on it? And Aphrodite knew which bow it was?"

"Did I hear my name? Are we talking about archery?" Looking absolutely fabulous in her off-the-shoulder designer gown, Aphrodite joined the group.

Eros gave her a confused look. "Mom, did you shoot Nina and Pan with one of my arrows?"

For a second Aphrodite looked guilty then she shrugged. "I guess this is a day for sharing secrets. I wanted to teach Nina a lesson about interfering with me, and Pan stepped in the way and got hit as well, that's all."

Eros closed his eyes for a moment. "I don't suppose that you'd guessed ahead of time that he might do that."

The goddess examined the polish on her perfect fingernails. "I might have suspected that he would step in front of the arrow. He always was a little protective of Nemesis and I suspected there might be more going on between them."

"But mother, you didn't tell them it was a practice arrow and you had to know. You gave me that set."

Aphrodite patted his cheek. "Well, of course I knew, sweetheart. I wouldn't aim one of your real bespelled arrows at anyone—that would be wrong!" She glanced mischievously at Nina and Pan. "But I knew what they didn't know wouldn't hurt them. And now look at them, happily married just as they should be."

Aphrodite's beaming smile took in everyone at the party. "So many happy couples, here," she sighed. "It's a shame Violet and Nick couldn't make it, since they were my first, but there is Chloe and Alex, and now Nina and Pan."

For a moment she eyed Astraios and Eos, the Titan couple near the refreshment table. The pair was arguing about something, but they were smiling all the time. A slight frown wrinkled the skin between her eyes. "They seem to be doing all right on their own, but giving them a little push wouldn't hurt..."

"Woman, I'm putting my foot down." Hep limped over and seized Aphrodite by the shoulders. He glared into her surprised face. "For months now Nina and Pan have been worried that the love they had wasn't real and would go away soon. If you'd told them before now that it was all them and not a spell they wouldn't have had to go through that." He gave her a little shake that dislodged some of her perfect coiffure, allowing a single strand of golden hair to snake down her face. Aphrodite's eyes crossed as she looked at the strand next to her nose.

Hep pushed the hair out of her face. "You've interfered for the last time. From now on the only love affair I want you involved with is ours." He dragged her to him and his lips covered hers in a passionate kiss that drew applause from everyone around. Even Eros looked impressed.

When they broke off, Aphrodite lay limp in her husband's arms. Hep tossed a grin at Pan, then gathered up his wife and threw her over his shoulder. The rest of her hair came down in a golden stream that fell across his back.

"I hope you don't mind, Pan, Nina," Hep told them. "Lovely wedding and all, but got some stuff to work out with the wife." He turned and made his way out of the garden.

Pan didn't even try to hide his snicker. "Think nothing of it, Hep. Good luck!" he called after them. "He'll need it," he added quietly to Nina once they were gone.

Eros convulsed with laughter. "I didn't know the old man had it in him. I guess Mom will have to be more careful from now on with her meddling." He grinned happily then sobered briefly as he glanced at Nina and Pan. "There is one thing you should know, though. There was one small spell on that arrow, just on its point."

He pointed to the heart-shaped pendant on her chest. "The arrowhead is a normal shape unless it hits someone who really is in love. Only then will it turn into a heart." He pointed at both Pan and Nina. "Since it hit both of you, I'd say you were both in love when it happened."

Eros placed his hands on both of their shoulders and it felt to Nina like a benediction—a divine blessing on their marriage from the god of love. She felt aglow with happiness.

"Congratulations to you both," he said. "You deserve your happy ending."

* * * * *

Well, Nina said to herself, *maybe you could end a sexually explicit story with a wedding after all.* She waited next to Pan as they said goodnight to the last of their guests. A short burst of air blew past them and then they were alone in the garden.

Pan looked at her and winked. *On the other hand,* Nina added to her previous thought, *adding a sexy wedding night wouldn't be amiss.* She winked back at him and watched the grin on his face widen.

"Hello, Mrs. Pan," he told her, gathering her into his arms. He rubbed his beard on the top of her head and glanced up at the moon and stars above. "Time for us to be in bed."

"I'm not very sleepy," she told him, nuzzling his neck.

"Good," he said, smiling broadly. "Neither am I."

He swept her up into his arms and strode toward the bower.

"I can walk," Nina told him, but he wasn't listening.

"I'm told this is what a man does, carry his new wife over the threshold. Has something to do with the Romans stealing women, or something like that. Something about the Sabine..."

He continued talking nonsense as he walked and Nina was laughing by the time they passed through the doorway. Pan set her down by the bed and kissed her tenderly, silencing her laugh and making her swoon again. He then pointed his fingers around the room. Scented candles burst into flame near the bed and on top of Nina's new chest of drawers. A bouquet of sweetly scented flowers appeared on the table near the new his and hers walk-in closets, further perfuming the air.

Shaking her head in wonder, Nina examined the transformed room in its romantic coziness. There really were a lot of advantages being married to a god, especially a god who knew how to set the stage for a really good seduction.

The candles, the flowers, the fresh black satin sheets she could now see peeking out of the covers on the bed, all of those were a surprise he'd cooked up for her. Of course, she had a few surprises coming for him tonight. Nina tried to keep from grinning openly at the thought of what she had in store for her new husband.

Pan shrugged his way out his tuxedo jacket and unbuttoned the matching vest, letting both fall to the floor, then undid his pants and dropped them on top of the rest. He waved his hand and all three disappeared, followed by his shirt. Nina looked down expecting to see him naked, only to be caught by surprise.

She giggled then laughed. "Oh, Pan."

With a devilish grin he glanced down at the bright red bikini thong that covered his genitals. "I figured I might as well join you in wearing underwear, at least for today." He drew her into his arms. "Besides, those tuxedo pants you had me wear were so tight, it was the only way I could keep from displaying my erection."

"You had an erection?" She hadn't really noticed.

"Oh yes. Every time I looked at you in that dress. All I could think of was how many people were around and how long I had to wait before I could get it off you." His face showed honest distress. "I'm not used to waiting that long for satisfaction."

"Oh, poor baby," Nina said with amused sympathy. She ran her hand along the ridge of his erection, now peeking above the edge of his underwear. "Maybe there is something that I can do to make it feel better."

In a moment she had the thong pushed aside and his cock in her mouth. She sucked him long and hard and he groaned under her gentle ministrations.

"Oh yes," Pan said through gritted teeth. "That's real good. You always have such a great mouth."

She grinned up at him, caressing his cock with her hand. "I always thought you said I was a mouthy wench."

Unperturbed, he grinned back at her. "That, too. Get back to it, wench!"

She did. With long strokes of her tongue she pulled him deep inside her, laving the head and shaft with her lips. One hand cupped his heavy balls through the thong, giving them a gentle massage that had him gasping for breath. Through gritted teeth Pan gave her half-heard instructions for what he wanted.

Nina didn't really need to hear him to know what to do. She knew what Pan wanted without him saying a word. Eventually his words were less directional and more merely expressive of appreciation. His hands cupped the back of her head, his long fingers slipping through her loose hair, clenching against her scalp.

Soon she felt the clench of his imminent release into her mouth. She pulled back from him. "Want me to stop?"

Pan grabbed her head and pulled her back onto his cock. "Not on your life."

He came in her mouth, spurting hot and hard against the back of her throat, and Nina swallowed it, its taste so special. It tasted of Pan.

Pan's cum acted like a love potion for her and made her hot with desire, the sensation pooling deep inside her and flooding her core. Pan pulled her up off her knees and kissed her, sharing in the taste of his cum on her tongue.

"Don't worry, wife, there is plenty more where that came from." He grinned at his pun. "But here I am, naked, and you're still completely dressed. That doesn't seem fair."

He examined her gown and its elaborate fastenings. "I suppose you like this garment, right?" he asked, obviously hoping he could simply tear it off her.

At her nod, he sighed, but then began working the straps that held up the gown at the shoulders. He was surprised when they parted easily and the gown fell away to the floor.

"Oh, Nina," Pan breathed, his voice hushed by astonishment.

She glanced down at the surprise she'd rigged up for him. Instead of her usual attractive but simple underwear,

Nina and Chloe had found something a little different to see if Pan couldn't be coaxed out of his antipathy toward underwear.

Her bright red undergarments consisted of a strapless bustier that supported and lifted, but did not cover her breasts. The garment left her pebbled nipples and their dark areolas open to Pan's gaze, not to mention his hands and lips. Pan's mouth seemed to water at the sight of her luscious orbs so available for him to sample.

She stepped a little bit away and spread her legs slightly, and now he could see that the matching panties were crotchless with just the littlest edge of lace running along the inside of her legs. He could see her nether lips with their closely cropped dark hair, peeking through the gap.

Pan threw his hands in the air. "I give in. Nina, that is the most beautiful underwear I've ever seen."

She laughed. "It's all for you, Pan."

Lifting her into his arms, he laid her on the bed. "You are all for me, Nina. And I'm all for you." A hint of seriousness touched the amusement and passion in his eyes. "And that's how it's going to be between us."

"No argument from me, Pan." She stroked his face and tugged playfully on his beard. "Let's make love."

*****

Pan covered her with his body, but didn't join with her at once. She was his now all his, for now and for always. No longer did he have to worry about losing her, about her leaving him as soon as the spell was over.

Now they knew there never had been a spell in the first place, no magic except for what they made together. Pan smiled. Nina loved him. She really loved him.

For a moment he thought of the wasted years, when they'd been apart, but he had to be philosophical about it. Would they have appreciated the miracle of their love if they hadn't spent so much time apart? Would it be the same for them now, or would they not have realized the specialness of what they had?

Pan liked to think that what was between them now was worth the waiting and sacrifices they'd both made to achieve it. Certainly he would never take for granted having Nina in his life.

For once he didn't remove her very decorative underwear but left it in place as he devoted his mouth to her breasts, laving each nipple with a skill that left her breathless. When she was writhing from that, he turned his attention to the delicate parts of her sweet little pussy, still peeking at him from its lacy covering. He liked the feel of the lace against his cheeks as he dove in to taste her honeyed pussy, covered in her rich arousal. So sweet, so special. So…Nina.

Pan smiled. His Nina, his Nemesis, but she'd never really been his enemy. She was just the woman he needed to complete him and make him whole. As she lay under him she moaned aloud, her hands clutched at his horns, holding them and using them to direct him into her pussy.

He ate her until she wept for him to stop, pulling on his horns to bring him up her body to where she could kiss him and taste herself on his lips. Pan fitted his cock to her pussy, arching over her while still kissing her.

When Pan finally drove his hard cock into her it made them complete, a single entity, a couple, god and wife. Part of that was the joining of two bodies into a whole—the rest was the singularity of how they felt for each other. He pulled back and drove in again and Nina cried out her pleasure at his stroke.

What a wonderful sound, Pan thought. Nina clutched at him and the rake of her nails on his back was wonderful. She bit his shoulder and tightened her legs hard around his waist and it was all wonderful, wonderful. Anything she did was wonderful since Nina was his and that made it wonderful.

He couldn't help his happy grin as he took possession of her body and her sweet, sweet pussy. All of it his, forever and forever. She continued to rake his back, scream her joy, and meet each of his strokes with one of her own.

In spite of having already come in Nina's mouth, Pan couldn't hold off his need to climax again much longer. He tried, but Nina writhed beneath him, her body on fire and it felt like his cock pistoning into her was the only thing keeping her from bursting into flames. He used it to drive her into a screaming orgasm, his name a part of her cry. As her scream died in his ears, he put off his own satisfaction no longer and climaxed again with a sturdy cry of his own.

He wasn't finished yet, though. Pulling out of her, he turned her over and entered her from behind, his cock still rock-hard. The edge was off of his need and now he could take his time and make their loving memorable. He kept his strokes long and slow, and Nina moaned her appreciation.

She glanced back over her shoulder, her smile sensuous, then closed her eyes as her pussy tightened again around his cock, the ripples milking him. He nearly halted, not wanting to finish again so quickly, but Nina pushed back into him, forcing him to continue.

"Don't stop, Pan. PLEASE!" Her cries finished when another long rippling orgasm slid through her. Again she tightened and Pan gasped at how firmly she gripped his cock, deeply buried inside her.

He couldn't help it. He had to come again, and this time he knew it would be the finish for him. Pan sped up, pounding against Nina's backside. His cock was so hot it felt like it was on fire. He could barely hold back finishing.

"NINA!" He gasped out her name as she collapsed underneath him. Pan pulled her back up into his arms and kissed the back of her neck while continuing to stroke deep inside her.

Turning her head, Nina rubbed her soft cheek against him. He felt her pussy clutch his cock again, a sure sign she was close to another climax. "Come with me, Pan," she gasped out. "Like a couple…" her voice trailed off.

Still supporting her weight he drove deep inside, one hand now stroking her clit. Nina bucked back against him and he couldn't hold off finishing any longer.

They came at the same time, simultaneous cries of passion echoing off the bower walls. Passion sated, they collapsed onto the bed and for a while only the sound of their labored breathing could be heard.

Nina turned to face Pan, her small hands framing his face. She looked so serious that a pang of concern slipped through him, but that vanished with her words.

"I love you, Pan." She fondled his tiny horns. "I always have, you know."

"I'm not sure when I started loving you," he told her. "Maybe it was when we first were together. Maybe it was after you walked out on me. It doesn't matter anymore, when you loved me or I loved you, so long as you love me today, tomorrow, and for the rest of time. And I'll promise you the same."

"'The rest of time'?" she repeated, her smile returning. "That's quite a while."

"Not nearly long enough for a god to love his wife."

"Very well then. For the rest of time will be how long I love you."

"For the rest of time," he repeated and they sealed the bargain with a kiss.

Later he held his wife close as she slept, her body free of the bits of decorative cloth she'd called underwear. For once he hadn't torn or disintegrated her garments, but allowed her to take them off as they'd been intended to be removed so they could be worn later.

Pan slid one hand down her silky thigh, enjoying the smoothness under his hand. She murmured something quietly in her sleep and rubbed her foot down the fleece covering his leg. The action seemed to sooth her and she fell deeper into slumber.

Suddenly Pan remembered the sheepskin-covered pillow in the bed in her apartment, the one she said she used to sleep with. It was all he could do not to laugh out loud. Nina, the fierce vengeance nymph, had missed him so much after they'd broken up that she'd taken to sleeping with a pillow against her legs as a substitute. Perhaps someday he'd tell her that he'd figured it out. They had plenty of time to learn each other's secrets now.

He smiled. *The rest of time.*

Pan kissed the back of her neck and let her sweet smell soothe him and ease him toward his own slumber. Sleeping together, like making love, was part of being a couple, a wonderful part, but not the only part. There would be good times and bad, he knew, and issues would come up that they would have to work through.

But there would be laughter and joy as well, and things they would do together, both in and out of the bedroom.

Nina was his wife and he was her husband. They were a couple, now and always, joined by law, but in heart and spirit as well. And that's the way it would be for the rest of time.

Pan smiled, and with that last thought closed his eyes and fell asleep.

The End

Enjoy this excerpt from

Memories to Come

"You're a soldier, Remak. All you've known is war and destruction, all you've experienced is hate. You've fought for your people, but you've never loved for them."

Anger filled him, wiping away his fear. "That's who I am, what I am."

"Yes, but it didn't have to be that way. You had a choice, once. You could have known love."

That gave him pause as an old memory crept to the surface of his mind. How could she know?

Again she answered as if he'd spoken his thoughts. "How could I not? I gave you that chance, placed that woman where you would find her. Do you even remember her?"

A shiver passed through him, this time not one of fear but desire. *He remembered.* It had been years ago, but he remembered the woman who'd made him think of something other than war, imagine a life without fighting.

He'd met her during one of the many skirmishes he'd participated in. She was a village woman some men from another part of his army had taken captive. That happened sometimes when the army moved through a village—one of the reasons soldiers weren't always welcome.

The men had planned to rape her, but when he'd seen her with them, Remak couldn't let that happen. He'd fought them and freed her…then let her go.

Remak stared at the goddess before him, now realizing how familiar she was. The village woman had looked like her, with copper skin and hair the color of autumn leaves. Green eyes, too, but Remak remembered them as a warm green, warm with admiration and gratitude when he'd cut her free. Warm with desire as well. He'd held her for only a brief moment, too brief, but he remembered how she'd melted in his arms. His cock hardened at the memory.

"You let her go, freed her," the goddess said. "Kept her safe from the other men. But you didn't stay with her in her village and you should have."

Duty had forced him to go, but it had been hard not to remain behind with her. For weeks afterward his thoughts had strayed to the woman with the peaceful green eyes and hair like flame. It had taken all his discipline not to abandon his post and seek her out.

But he'd fought the urge, and eventually the need to be with her had faded. Even when he'd finally served his time and was released from service, he'd rejoined immediately rather than return to the little village that had been her home.

Remak met the goddess's icy glare. "She wasn't my woman. I couldn't..."

"She could have been. She was destined to be."

The goddess was so certain. How could he argue with her? Maybe she was right, and he had passed up a chance to be a man with a family and a home.

No, Remak argued with himself. He hadn't made the wrong decision. He wasn't suited to be such a man. He doubted that he could ever have been satisfied with having a wife. After all, he'd had many women in his lifetime and never wanted one more than once or twice. How could one woman be enough for any man?

Again the goddess seemed to read his mind. "One woman is more than enough, if she's the right woman."

Remak doubted that. Still, what good did it do him now? He was a prisoner dying in a cell and he'd never taste freedom again, much less enjoy a woman's embrace.

He couldn't speak more on it. "What use is this?" he growled. "I'm to die here."

The goddess shook her head. "As I said, I'm here to offer redemption. A chance to see what your life would have been like had you taken advantage of that opportunity."

"Why me?"

"Because you are strong, yet you never took advantage of that. You never used your strength or position to violate others."

It was true he'd never participated in rape during his career as a soldier, nor taken anything not offered freely. He'd heard the others mutter about him for that, but rape and pillaging had never appealed to him. Forcing someone to service him hadn't felt…right.

"And that's why I'm here, Remak, because you never took what wasn't given." The goddess nodded at him. "Do you accept my deal?"

"What deal can we have?" He shook the chains above him. "I'm not going anywhere."

The goddess eyed the chains with amused contempt then shrugged her shoulders as if they weren't important. "Then you will do what I wish. You will learn what a man who worships me knows. Learn from the experiences I give you."

In spite of himself, he was curious. "How?"

With her cold smile, the goddess came close enough to touch him…but didn't. She raised her hand to hover in front of his face.

"It's quite simple. Just close your eyes."

About the author:

Cricket Starr lives in the San Francisco Bay area with her husband of more years than she chooses to count. She loves fantasies, particularly sexual fantasies, and sees her writing as an opportunity to test boundaries. Her driving ambition is to have more fun than anyone should or could have. While published in other venues under her own name, she's found a home for her erotica writing here at Ellora's Cave.

Cricket welcomes mail from readers. You can write to her c/o Ellora's Cave Publishing at 1056 Home Ave. Akron, Oh. 44310-3502.

Why an electronic book?

We live in the Information Age—an exciting time in the history of human civilization in which technology rules supreme and continues to progress in leaps and bounds every minute of every hour of every day. For a multitude of reasons, more and more avid literary fans are opting to purchase e-books instead of paperbacks. The question to those not yet initiated to the world of electronic reading is simply: *why?*

1. *Price.* An electronic title at Ellora's Cave Publishing and Cerridwen Press runs anywhere from 40-75% less than the cover price of the exact same title in paperback format. Why? Cold mathematics. It is less expensive to publish an e-book than it is to publish a paperback, so the savings are passed along to the consumer.
2. *Space.* Running out of room to house your paperback books? That is one worry you will never have with electronic novels. For a low one-time cost, you can purchase a handheld computer designed specifically for e-reading purposes. Many e-readers are larger than the average handheld, giving you plenty of screen room. Better yet, hundreds of titles can be stored within your new library—a single microchip. (Please note that Ellora's Cave and Cerridwen Press does not endorse any specific brands. You can check our website at www.ellorascave.com or

www.cerridwenpress.com for customer recommendations we make available to new consumers.)

3. *Mobility*. Because your new library now consists of only a microchip, your entire cache of books can be taken with you wherever you go.
4. *Personal preferences are accounted for*. Are the words you are currently reading too small? Too large? Too...**ANNOYING**? Paperback books cannot be modified according to personal preferences, but e-books can.
5. *Instant gratification*. Is it the middle of the night and all the bookstores are closed? Are you tired of waiting days—sometimes weeks—for online and offline bookstores to ship the novels you bought? Ellora's Cave Publishing sells instantaneous downloads 24 hours a day, 7 days a week, 365 days a year. Our e-book delivery system is 100% automated, meaning your order is filled as soon as you pay for it.

Those are a few of the top reasons why electronic novels are displacing paperbacks for many an avid reader. As always, Ellora's Cave and Cerridwen Press welcomes your questions and comments. We invite you to email us at service@ellorascave.com, service@cerridwenpress.com or write to us directly at: 1056 Home Ave. Akron OH 44310-3502.

THE ELLORA'S CAVE LIBRARY

Stay up to date with Ellora's Cave Titles in Print with our Quarterly Catalog.

TO RECIEVE A CATALOG,
SEND AN EMAIL WITH YOUR NAME
AND MAILING ADDRESS TO:

CATALOG@ELLORASCAVE.COM

OR SEND A LETTER OR POSTCARD
WITH YOUR MAILING ADDRESS TO:

CATALOG REQUEST
C/O ELLORA'S CAVE PUBLISHING, INC.
1337 COMMERCE DRIVE #13
STOW, OH 44224

ELLORA'S CAVE
ROMANTICA PUBLISHING